C000171635

It Came from the Sky

R. E. Smith

For Mrs. Wells,

the one who helped me get into this mess.

Acknowledgments

Thank you to the friends who have helped me make sure this journey makes sense. Without you, I would've gone absolutely mad by now.

Chapter One

With the birds flying above me, the trees swaying in the breeze, and the river moving smoothly beside me, it's hard to imagine this as one of the hottest days of the year. Yet here I am, sweating through my work clothes and panting like an animal. Today is a Scavenging Day, which means all of the able women in the village must lend a hand in order for us to have food. It's supposed to be an important rite, hand chosen for us by the gods of old. Atzi, my closest friend, says it's just a story the first Chief told the women to get them to stay out of the men's way. Even when I call her a betrayer of the faith, I can't bring myself not to believe her.

My mother's instructions are clear in my head: *go find Atzi, she's late.* My pleading only moments later is also still clear: *by myself? I can't go into the forest alone.* Naturally, here I am: in the forest, alone. Some people call the birds flying above peaceful, but I can only see shadows ready to swoop down and attack. Trees swaying in the breeze look more like clawed hands reaching out to me. The only peace of mind I have is the gurgling of the river, bringing with it a promise of safety and home. It's the river that leads the women to the Scavenging Fields and brings the men home after long hunting trips. Where the forest is known to take men from their families, the river will always bring them back.

I walk in the middle of a beaten path worn down by my ancestors. The path itself is a small strip of earth -- brown and lifeless, but it always manages to bring us back home after long days spent gathering food. Thinking of home reminds me of my mother; the thought of the task before me makes me sigh. Here I am, walking in the hottest weather the village has seen in years to go get Atzi, who must know she's in trouble for making me walk through the forest alone. Why else would she intentionally avoid going to the Scavenging Field late, if not to make me face my fears as she always seems to do? *She must think she's helping me,* I reason, *she must think I'm too scared and not a good enough liar for some adventure she has planned.*

As any friend would, I told my mother that Atzi must have gotten sidetracked helping Zolin, the eldest son of the Chief. Of course, I also knew that this must be a lie because, though Atzi and Zolin often talk to each other, they very rarely say anything nice. Atzi will call Zolin some name or make fun of his position as the eldest son of the Chief. Zolin will retaliate by calling Atzi crazy or out of favor with the gods. I can always see that Zolin is joking, trying to lighten the fact that Atzi absolutely means what she says. As much as I adore that girl, I can't help but have a feeling that she will get us both in trouble with the village one day, talking to the son of the Chief like that. I can already see my father shaking his head, repeating the words he has told me since the day I met Atzi: *That child's a wild one, Mila. Be careful with her.*

As I'm walking, a bird perches on a low-lying branch, making me jump with its quick movements. The bird is singing a song -- some kind of buzzing melody -- but the forest is already so loud with the river nearby that I can't hear a thing. The bird cocks its head to the side, and for a moment I think back to the stories of my childhood, the stories of the gods. So many tales are dedicated to the gods coming down transformed into animals to test the faith of the people they created. *If this is a god,* I think, *then I hope he isn't disappointed in my lack of bravery.* Before I can do something ridiculous, like asking the bird its name or running away, an arrow comes flying past, making me nearly dive for the cover of the trees next to me. The arrow is too far to the right, missing both the bird and the tree he was happily seated in. Despite missing the bird, the arrow nearly soars through me, filling my body with the energy needed to make a quick jump to safety. As the bird flies off in fright, I look for the poorly trained Hunter, wanting to make sure that I won't be shot at again. There, hiding in a tree of his own, is Necalli, the youngest son of the Chief.

I'm not afraid of this child, he's too young to be the fearsome hunter I was imagining. "Were you aiming for me or the bird?" I ask, using deep breaths to try to get the adrenaline out of my system.

Necalli is too far away for me to see much, but I don't hear him laugh. "I would've had him earlier if you hadn't scared him off with your loud footsteps."

Necalli was a young spitfire, always trying to prove himself from the moment you met him. Out of respect for his family, I keep my mouth shut from some spiteful remark. Better to stay in favor with the Chief then risk angry glares from the village for the rest of my life. "I hope you find another bird," I said. I began walking the path again, following the beaten earth in the direction of Necalli. "Should you be hunting by yourself?"

"Zolin is too busy helping the other boys. I'm getting in practice. I'm too old to be relearning kids' stuff. And the forest isn't scary for men like me."

There was a tempting thought of pointing out that Necalli may still need his brother's advice, but I pushed the thought away, "I'll leave you to it, then. Good luck."

Necalli said nothing but began hopping through the trees like he himself were a bird looking for a new place to perch. I rolled my eyes. *I don't remember Zolin being so conceited as a child.* I picked up my earlier pace, hoping no more stray arrows would come close to me again. As I went on, I found myself continuing to dodge the failed archery attempts of Necalli, who, it seems, had been hunting for a while now. Shaking my head, I started picking up his forgotten arrows. Maybe giving these to Zolin would make him see that his brother needed some extra attention. Some more supervision wouldn't hurt too much, either.

Picking up the arrows gave me something to focus on, so I made good time returning to the village. Of course, by that time, I had half a quiver of arrows, and I could just make out Zolin teaching the younger kids in the outskirts of the village. *Maybe now he'll try to put some more effort into his brothers training.* Necalli could certainly put it to good use.

As I neared the training grounds, which was on the outskirts of the village leading to the Scavenging Field, I studied the children in attendance. They were all much younger than me -- maybe seven or eight -- but they were skilled for their age. Today must've been an archery day because they were all shooting their arrows at targets hung to nearby trees. Their aim wasn't great, but their posture was nearly perfect. All courtesy, naturally, of the best hunter in the village.

Zolin was standing over his disciples, analyzing them as an instructor would. He had the regal walk of a Chief, back straight and face expressionless. Yet when he leaned over to whisper in the ears of the younger boys, they didn't seem frightened or intimidated. In that aspect, he was much like his mother; approachable and kind. I watched him fix how one of the boys notched their arrows before I walked over, unsure of myself in a field full of children amateurly holding weapons.

"Zolin," I said, announcing my presence and getting his attention. I held up the arrows, "One of your students might need some more target practice."

"Necalli?" He asked, "Did he not at least grab the arrows after he shot them?" Zolin shook his head, taking Necalli's strays from my hands, "He didn't shoot you, did he?"

"Near miss." I joked, "How are these kids doing?"

Zolin puffed out his chest, taking pride in his students, "Good. In a few years, we'll have some good hunters for the village."

"That's great." I agreed. Zolin helped the boy closest to us with his grip on the bow before turning back to me. "It's good that these boys are training under the finest Hunter in the village. They'll be as good as the gods by the time you're through with them."

Zolin looked down, smiling but also shaking his head, "The finest Hunter this village ever saw was your father. I'm just passing on the wisdom I managed to learn from him."

My father was once a Hunter in the village like Zolin. Some said he was the best Hunter in the village, but I never knew him that way. Before I was born, he was in an accident that nearly took his life. Mother said she prayed to the gods all night for my father to be safe. In the end, he was alive, but too injured to continue hunting. Now he helps make weapons for the Hunters -- bows, arrows, and spears.

"That's kind of you to say," I said. A breeze blew through the field, blowing hair into my eyes. I tucked the hair behind my ear before continuing, "You haven't seen Atzi, have you?"

Zolin nodded his head, "It's a Scavenging Day, isn't it?"

"And I'm kind of in a hurry."

Zolin looked back toward the village, "I saw her by the river on the other side of the village. She was helping some animal."

"Sounds like her." I agreed, "Thank you."

"It's no problem at all." I turned to walk toward the river before Zolin caught my attention again. "Mila?"

"Yes?"

"If you see Necalli again, tell him to meet me for training."

"Of course."

The village was mostly silent today, what with the women in the Scavenging Field and the younger sons training. All that was left were the older Elites and the young daughters, most of which seemed to be helping the elderly women weave baskets. It's a tradition amongst our people that the younger girls learn their skills from the most experienced in the village. It teaches the children respect and the Elders about change, or, at least, that's what my mother told me.

Jumping over a rolling basket that must've been tossed in frustration, I looked around for Atzi, hoping she would make herself known soon so we could get to work. With each house I passed, I took in the emptiness that was radiating from inside. Every villager seemed busy today. Through the silence, I became more sure that Atzi was still by the river, completely lost in her own world. Atzi's house was the first familiar house that I passed, and it was lifeless with both of its inhabitants gone. Not long after that, I passed my house, which was quiet too. *I'm sure Father is still sleeping.* I thought about checking in on him but figured his disappointment that I wasn't working would overcome any joy in seeing me without reason.

The path to the river isn't far from my house. It is a slick and often muddy trail, so I took my time navigating the bends, steps, and loose tree roots that were liable to trip up even the most experienced pathfinder. I knew where Atzi was; I could picture it in my mind: the place where we spent most of our childhood playing. It's a little clearing by the river where the trees aren't as thick and the current isn't as strong. There are rocks leading right by the water, and trees that are big but easy to climb. It's peaceful, secluded, and lets the mind run wild. Whenever we could sneak away, this was where we'd go.

It took several more steps before I was close. If I listened above the sounds of the rushing river beside me, I could just make out a voice up ahead. Though it wasn't very clear, I knew it was my friend. Who else would come all the way out here just to be alone? No one else in the village had a mind that worked like Atzi's. Another bend in the path and I was in the clearing. Sure enough, there was Atzi with a bird in her hands. She seemed to be feeding it some grains, but I couldn't tell if the bird was injured or not. *Just like her to tame another pet.*

"What happened to this one?" I asked. "It looks too old for it to be lost."

Atzi hardly stirred, as if she knew I was coming. "I saved him from a snake, but he's startled. I'm calming him down."

"He's a bird. I don't think he can feel startled or calm."

"That's a lie." Atzi made no move from her position on the ground, so I decided to join her instead. "Can you see his eyes? See how wide and afraid they are?"

I couldn't see anything wrong with the bird, but that wasn't unusual for me. "You're late for work."

"I'm saving his life." She said, gesturing to the bird, "This is far more important."

"Our mothers don't think so. They're angry."

"They're always angry."

"You're always late."

"I'm the only one who cares about these little guys."

Either the bird sensed our argument or was tired of being held because he began moving as if preparing to fly away. Atzi sensed this and moved her hands upward to give him some speed. The bird flew away to a nearby branch before perching and pruning his feathers.

"You scared him away," Atzi complained. "I wasn't finished fixing him yet."

"I will never be finished fixing you if we don't get to work soon." I countered.

Instead of retorting with some quip or snarky remark, Atzi turned and smiled at me. "All right, you win. But only if you cover for me."

"If anyone asks, you were helping Zolin retrieve the lost arrows of the young hunters."

"I'd say you were sent by the gods if I believed in them."

Atzi jumped away before I could smack her arm. I stood up after her, and we began the long walk back to the Scavenging Field. "You shouldn't say that."

"In whose company? Yours or the birds?" She teased, nodding her head back to the feathered creature still perched in the tree.

"Anyone. If the gods are listening, you could be the next poor villager who gets turned into some strange creature as a punishment."

"Wouldn't that be fun? Mother would be so proud!"

I grinned. It was true that Atzi's mother wasn't the most thoughtful woman when it came to her daughter. She wasn't neglectful, she just has a specific vision in mind. One that boosted the position of her daughter and herself. Some would call her delusional or harsh, but others would just call her driven. That's how Atzi and I see her: a woman obsessed with remedying her position with the village. Atzi didn't care anymore -- once her father left, he was practically dead in her eyes -- but Atzi's mother never recovered. That's why we never bring it up, and never think too much about Atzi's mother's decisions.

We walked the rest of the way to the village in silence, but it was a comfortable one. I eventually noticed Atzi studying the things around her -- the grass, trees, flowers, and clouds. I don't know how she never got bored of it all. I commented on this, but she only laughed.

"You do the same thing with your star watching."

I laughed, "At least the stars change and move. The only reason the trees move is the wind or the men cutting them down."

"It's different. You just have to pay attention."

"I have. You've made me."

"You just don't have an open mind," she insisted. "One of these days you'll learn."

"And then what?" I asked.

Atzi turned around to face me, walking backward as she did, "You'll--"

Before I could warn her, she ran into a tall woman with dark hair. Only Atzi fell to the ground, which was a blessing from the gods as the woman turned out to be--

"Etapalli!" Atzi exclaimed. Thankfully, Atzi had the good sense to get on her knees with her head bowed in respect to the Chief's wife, "My apologies."

"It's all right, child." Etapalli laughed, a natural sound that rivaled bird songs. "Are you hurt?"

"No, ma'am." Atzi got up and I moved to stand beside her. "Sorry for running into you."

"How are you, girls?" Etapalli asked, "It's been too long since I've seen you."

Etapalli is not just the wife of the Chief and mother of Zolin and Necalli, she's also the only teacher for the children of the village. She sees all the children and teaches them about the gods and our history. When we were children, we compared her to the women typically pictured in our legends of the gods -- beautiful, compassionate, and fearless. She's the woman every child has dreamed of being. Of course, she hasn't taught the young girls in the village since we were small, but even now she teaches and men the younger boys.

"We're doing well." I chimed in, noticing the red that's appearing on Atzi's face. "We're heading to work now."

"You mean Scavenging? Aren't you a little late?" She teased.

At this, Atzi turned even redder, and I laughed to try and ease some of the tension away, "Yes, miss."

"Well, I won't keep you any longer. I'm sure the other women are waiting for you."

"Yes, ma'am." Atzi and I said in unison.

We hurried along after that, me holding in laughter and Atzi holding in an angry retort concerning my laughter. It wasn't until after we passed Zolin -- who Atzi angrily stared at when he tried to say hello to us -- that Atzi finally mustered up the evil glare she had envisioned giving me earlier. In the uneasy silence of the forest, she truly did look like an evil villager whom the gods were sent in to control. When I told her this, she only huffed in annoyance.

"Leave it to you to let me embarrass myself in front of the Chief's wife."

"On the bright side," I said, "at least you can tell the women that we were talking to Etapalli. That's an even greater reason to miss work."

"How lucky we are that my clumsiness has saved us once again." I couldn't miss the sarcasm in her voice.

"Yes, praise the gods."

"Oh, hush," Atzi said, "before I curse you with powers so evil that the gods themselves could not rival them."

Chapter Two

The Scavenging Field is a section of forest surrounded by trees bearing fruits and bushes full of berries. Sometimes there are beehives in the trees, and the women work together to knock them down for their honey. Nearby is a runoff stream from the river, which the women use to get drinks, cool off, and wash off the food gathered before we return home. Though the grass is trampled and the ground well worn by the footsteps of our ancestors, the forest is still thick with trees and vines. The younger children were always watched when they first came to the Field because it was just as dangerous here as it was anywhere else in the forest.

By the time we reached the Scavenging Field, many more women besides our mothers were scowling at us. Atzi and I exchanged looks as they turned their backs to us, refusing to acknowledge us until we explained why we were so late to work. Explaining our encounter with Zolin and Etapalli helped, but even then, my mother thought it best to whisper advice in my ear.

"You two better work hard today, Mila."

"We will," I assured her.

I said this before knowing it would be one of the hottest days we've seen in a long time. Even in the morning, when it was supposed to be cool, many of us were already sweating heavily. Each family of women had brought something to hold their drinking water, which was easily drained before midday. Atzi and I, as two of the youngest who still had some experience with work, were often told by our Elders to refill their cups and pots with water from the stream. Once or twice Atzi and I would wade deeper than necessary into the stream -- anything to cool off for even a moment.

It somehow felt as if the day was stretching on, that it would never end at all, and we'd be stuck in the Scavenging Field for all eternity. I told this to my mother, who smiled at me.

"You have an active imagination, Mila." She said.

Atzi's mother, who overheard my complaints, turned to face us. "Or maybe the gods are playing tricks on us."

"Why would they," Mother asked, "when they have far more important duties like pulling the sun across the sky or telling the story of the eagle's wings so the rain may come?"

"Maybe they are growing bored waiting in the clouds. They haven't talked with our people in generations."

My mother shrugged, scolding Atzi and me for slowing down in our work before speaking to Atzi's mother again, "The wicked gods are locked far away. Our gods would never hurt us."

Several women nearby agreed with my mother before adding their thoughts to the discussion. I found it nauseating how quickly the ladies bickered in the dizzying heat. They brought up stories of the gods I hadn't heard since the days when Etapalli was my teacher, and recalled facts about stories I couldn't even remember. Atzi made faces the entire time, which almost got me in more trouble with the ladies for laughing -- I had to hold my breath to stifle the sound.

It wasn't much longer until the elder women called for a break. The younger kids were getting red from the sun, and most cups had been drained too quickly after Atzi and I filled them. We sat by the stream, our feet cooling off in the rushing water. Some of the younger children began splashing around, and, for a while, Atzi joined them while I helped my mother prepare a small meal for the tired workers.

We couldn't eat much of our spoils, but what we could spare felt as if it did wonders to restore our energy. Atzi and I sat off by ourselves, trading our unwanted food with each other and sharing what we wanted most. I had just finished my apple and was about to throw the core into the stream when I noticed Atzi looking around with a strange expression on her face.

"What's wrong?" I asked.

She stopped looking around, but still had that look on her face. "It's nothing."

"No, tell me." I insisted. "Even if it's about the birds."

I thought a little joking would calm her down, but her expression didn't change. "But it *is* about the birds."

"Then tell me. I won't laugh."

Atzi sighed, then turned to face me as if she was simultaneously working up her courage. "Don't you think it's pretty quiet here?"

I thought about the chirping birds, the laughing children, the scolding mothers, and the rushing stream beside us. I answered quickly, "No."

"Are you sure?" She asked.

I thought I was just going to humor her. I listened again, hearing the sounds of children, mothers, and the stream. But then I listened even closer. The wind was blowing hard, rustling the trees in a way that I hadn't noticed before. It was as if a storm was approaching even though the sun was shining brightly and there weren't many clouds in the sky. Listening for birds was useless because they seemed to have vanished. It was as if they had flown south for the winter, even though they wouldn't be departing until summer was over. No birdsongs could be heard, and while I had previously attributed that to the loudness of our group, looking around proved that no birds were near our group at all. It gave the forest a deathly, lifeless quality that I struggled to suppress.

"I'm sure we scared them off," I reasoned, shaking my head and facing resolutely toward the stream. "We aren't being quiet here."

"They've been gone for a while." Atzi insisted, but she said it so quietly that I pretended I couldn't hear her.

After some time spent in silence, my mother came over to sit beside us. She had a smile on her face and the remains of berries could be seen in her stained hands. "Thank you for helping the others."

"Anything for them to not glare at us," Atzi said, a smile back on her face.

"They're not mad at you." My mother insisted. "It's good of you to help the Chiefs' family. It shows good potential and character. You're representing the gods well."

Atzi shrugged off the compliment. "You sound like my mother."

I laughed to break the silence, but even then, it didn't sound very convincing. "Do you think a storm is coming? Atzi said the birds are very quiet."

My mother looked around, coming up with the same conclusion I had. "Some of the children were saying they wondered where the animals went. Maybe it will rain tomorrow. We haven't been blessed with rain in a long time."

Atzi nodded absently, "Maybe that's it."

"As long as it isn't a big storm," I added, remembering the last storm that had blown through the village. It had been a few days before summer started, and it had lasted two full days. By the time we could all safely leave our houses, many had been close to running low on food. Trees had fallen over, a few houses had been destroyed, and we almost had to replant a new Scavenging Field. "I don't want to spend another day picking up fallen branches for as long as I live."

Atzi nodded in agreement while my mother smiled. "That was a message from the gods. We won't see anything like that in my lifetime again."

Atzi and I shared a look which my mother seemed oblivious to. Before any religious conversation could come up -- a conversation in which Atzi would've had to politely excuse herself -- the Elders of the group called us all back to work. We stood up slowly -- a mix of the pressures of sitting on our legs and our unhappiness with being called back to work so soon. As we walked back to the Field, my mother stood in between me and Atzi, an arm around each of our shoulders.

"It won't be much longer before they give out," My mother quietly assured us. "They can't take as much of the heat as we can."

"Do you promise?" Atzi asked, bringing a smile to our faces.

"On the gods." She replied.

I would like to say that getting back to work was easier this time, now that we were all refreshed and energized. If anything, we were all less willing to work than before. Sitting and eating had made us tired, and we all seemed to be sweating even more now that we were moving again. Atzi and I began spending less time scavenging and more time refilling the water of the particularly vulnerable. Countless times, I had to ask Atzi to check on women who was swaying or blinking heavily. We helped them sit down and stand again when they asked, and with each weary woman, I knew we wouldn't be working much longer.

The sun hadn't moved much farther along the sky before one of the eldest women sat down with a huff. "I'm through." She grunted, wiping the sweat off her forehead. "Let's just catch our breath and head back to the village."

We smiled and some of the children even cheered before collapsing on the ground, passing around water and trying desperately to wipe the sweat and hair out of our eyes. Atzi came over to me, laying on her back with her head turned skyward. She didn't say anything, but I could see how tired she was when she closed her eyes. My mother smiled, mouthing the words 'Don't wake her.' to me. I nodded my head in a silent agreement.

We were all panting so hard from the heat -- maybe that's why we didn't notice the stillness of the forest around us. It seemed everything except the nearby stream had gone silent, frozen in a perfect picture of the Field. Our breathing was so loud that, at first, I didn't think anything was wrong. The forest seemed, for the first time, peaceful and quiet with the talking women resting in the shade of the trees. I should've realized that the forest was too quiet. Quieter than I had ever heard it before.

It took awhile for the sound to grow loud enough to catch our attention: a buzzing sound, relatively low in pitch. At first, I thought it was the river, then maybe a signal from the village, but the sound persisted long past what the usual danger warning would've been. Not only had I had never heard a sound like this in my life, it was also coming from the unknown beyond the Scavenging Field, leading away from the safety of the village. Whatever this sound was, it was foreign.

The kids stopped playing with the grass at their feet, looking to their mothers for an answer to the mysterious buzzing. Mothers were looking to the Elders, searching for any sign that this wasn't anything out of the ordinary. The Elders were looking to each other, begging with their eyes for one of them to explain what was happening. In these few final moments of peace, the buzzing only grew louder.

Atzi sat up, looking to me with eyes wide. I only shook my head, as unsure as everyone else about the reverberations echoing throughout the forest. I moved closer to my mother and grabbed her hand for some comfort. She looked just as terrified as everyone else, an expression I had never seen before. I didn't like it. Her hands shook just like mine; her eyes darted around the forest, and she was tense -- as if ready to run off at any moment.

Then, as suddenly as the buzzing had started, I could see it. It was coming towards us through the forest, a shadow that coated the trees and the bushes in darkness. The buzzing was almost unbearable now, compared to the quiet we had worked in earlier. It moved slowly across the forest, steadily devouring the Scavenging Field. It was only when I saw some of the women pointing into the sky that I realized a shadow wasn't coming for us at all. It was much more dangerous than a shadow. It was something real.

What is that?

Chapter Three

I didn't know what was in the sky. In my motionless awe, I didn't move and my eyes stayed locked toward the unknown. This thing was something I'd never seen before: it was huge, taking up so much of my familiar blue sky. Dark in color, it looked as if the night had come early to destroy the day. Ignoring the deafening buzzing let me see a smooth body that, if it were blue, would probably blend right in with the sky. I wasn't afraid until I saw the others quickly stand, afraid of that Thing moving toward us with no sign of stopping.

"Mila. Run!" My mother yelled. She pulled me to my feet, grabbing onto my shoulders like I was her lifeline. "Go!"

We took off together hand in hand, and the rest of the women were not far behind. It took all of my willpower not to trip over the tree roots or tall grasses that stood between me and safety. The forest looked scarier than ever today, with tree branches reaching out to grab me and drag me back to the Thing in the sky. I could only think to run, run as fast as I could. I don't often pray to the gods with sincerity, but I found myself repeating in my head one word: *please.*

It was the sound of women screaming behind me that eventually reminded me that there were others just as frightened as me. I slowed down and let my mother guide me as I looked back. Atzi wasn't too far behind and was gaining speed. In my quick glances behind, I couldn't find Atzi's mother anywhere. Very few Elders were visible. Mothers pulling their children behind them blocked my eyes from much of the sight. When I saw the shadow of the Thing pass one of the mothers, I quickly turned forward again, pushing myself to go faster.

I could hear the cries of those in that Thing's shadow. "Monster," they were screaming. "Gods save us." Whether anything was happening to them or they were just afraid, I couldn't say. But I also knew I wasn't going to risk finding out for myself. If it was even possible, my grip on my mother tightened. We were running side by side now. Tears were running down our faces. Not even Atzi appearing by my side, finally catching up with us, could bring me any comfort.

In all our worrying, we forgot to watch our feet. My mother tripped, almost bringing me down with her. Atzi slowed several paces ahead of us. I could see the anxiousness on her face; she wanted to keep running like the wind. One look behind showed many other mothers thought the same thing. I didn't have time to pull my mother to her feet and regain our earlier speed, so I dragged us behind the safety of a tree, waiting for the stampede of women running by to pass. Atzi got the message and loyally waited for us behind a tree of her own.

We were panting like dogs from our run. I could feel a pain in my side. "You should go." My mother said, "Don't wait for me. I need to catch my breath."

"I'll catch my breath, too," I said. I grabbed her hand again, "It's fine."

One look in the direction of that Thing made it pretty clear that everything was not fine. We had outrun it for now, but it was still steadily making its way toward us. Some of the Elders were passing by us now. Their eyes showed determination, but I wondered how much of this their bodies could take. With each elder that passed, I could see even more tired distress. They weren't used to running for their lives. *Can they make it to the village?*

"We need to go," Atzi interrupted. She rushed over to my side, pulling my mother to her feet. "We can't wait here forever."

We were both holding my mother's hands now, taking off at a sprint to escape whatever was coming for us. When we had caught up with the Elders, my mother let go of our hands, moving to help the closest woman reach safety without straining her body. Atzi and I took the unspoken command and went to help other women who were lagging behind the group. That Thing was still looming behind us, creeping closer than I would like. Part of me thought of running, of taking off and saving myself. Only the grip of the elder beside me kept me in my place.

I almost thought we would never reach the village before I saw the familiar trees marking the upcoming clearing. I could hear shouting from the village, men commanding and comforting. It seemed to fill us all with energy, and even though we were the last to break the clearing we weren't last by much. Men, Warriors, came forward, taking the Elders from us. They began asking the Elders what was going on, telling them to report any information they had gathered. I walked toward the village with my face toward the Thing, trying to figure out what was happening. I could just see it trying to peek over the tops of the trees.

"Come on, Mila." My mother said, grabbing me by the elbow and pulling me closer to the village. We hadn't made it far before another hand grabbed my other arm. I jumped in alarm but was filled with relief when I saw Zolin's face.

"What's happening?" He asked, determination and fear equally written across his face. "Tell me what's going on."

"I'm not sure," I said quickly, eyes darting from his face to the trees. "I don't know."

"Tell me," he insisted, his grip tightening on my arm. I could still feel my mother's presence, wanting to move forward but not wanting to disrespect the son of the Chief. I didn't like this feeling taking over me.

"It came from the sky," I said. "There weren't any birds and there was buzzing and it came from the sky."

"From the gods?" He asked.

I shook my head, "I don't know."

He looked from my face to my mother, his grasp growing even tighter on my arm. He addressed my mother, "Go. I'll look after her. We need to know what's going on."

"What? No." Worry seared itself into my mother's face, and her grip on me grew equally tight.

"I'll take care of her." Zolin promised, "We just need to know what's going on. She's observant and I trust her. She can help us understand what's happening."

I could see the Thing growing closer, slowly but steadily. I didn't notice in my panic just how slow it was moving. It moved lazily, almost as if it was studying us before it would destroy us. *What is this thing?*

Zolin tugged on my arm, pulling me out of my mother's grip. If she had wanted to say no to him, she didn't have the chance now. Zolin merely nodded in her direction before dragging me away, back toward that Thing and the forest and the Warriors.

"Zolin--" I started, but he didn't let me finish.

He stopped just as we reached the first group of Warriors, hands on both of my shoulders and his face close to mine. "Tell us, Mila. What is this?"

I could see other Warriors looking at me eagerly as if my perspective could help them in some way. Why couldn't they just listen to the Elders? What had I seen that they hadn't?

"I don't know." I began again, "It's as dark as a raven and louder than the river after a flood. It moves slow but it doesn't stop." Suddenly a thought occurred to me, and I was ashamed it hadn't come to mind before, "Are the other women all right?"

"We're going out to make sure now." Someone behind me said. I turned, startled at the sound of a strong, deep voice. It was Zolin's father, the Chief. He was dressed for war with determination on every inch of his face.

Zolin's grip on me tightened, but his face never left his father. "What do we do?"

"Take this girl back to her family." The Chief instructed, "Then take some men and scout the perimeter of the village. Make sure our people will be safe." Zolin nodded and began leading me toward the village when the Chiefs' voice called for my attention.

We didn't stop walking, Zolin made sure of that, but I turned my head at the voice of the Chief. I had to. "Yes?"

He shouted now, "Thank you." He nodded, then turned back to his men. When he started giving orders, Zolin dragged my attention back in front of me.

I should've been pleased that the Chief complimented me, but too much fear was coursing through my body for any sense of pride to take over. I hardly noticed the three other Warriors following behind us, eyes trained towards the forest surrounding the village. I was suddenly very thankful Zolin never let go of me, because if he had, I probably would've collapsed and never made it home. I could feel my body shaking, which Zolin must have known as he gently pushed me forward.

"Thank you for helping us understand what's going on." He whispered. I nodded, but couldn't bring myself to say anything.

The village was deathly quiet. Windows were boarded up, doors were shut tight, and smoke from fires couldn't be seen. The only sounds were the commands of Warriors and the buzzing of that Thing still going strong. I stole a glance behind me, but couldn't see anything because of the trees and the Warriors' bodies towering behind me.

I tried to match my quick breathing to the beating of my heart, but both were too fast to bring any steadiness or comfort. I was torn between running home as fast as I could and throwing myself into the nearest hiding spot to wait out the wrath of this Thing. My eyes were darting from house to house, hoping to see any sign of life. *I don't like it. I don't like this.* The constant buzzing overpowered my ears and was driving me crazy.

I almost thought I'd never reach my house. My father opened the door quickly and I ran into his open arms.

"Thank you," He said to Zolin. I didn't hear any response; I was too busy running into my mother's arms. It's easy to cry in the safety of my house. It was even easier to match my hurried breathing to her much slower breaths.

I only heard my father close the door. He put an arm around each of us and led us to a corner of our house that is not near the door or window. We sat together wrapped in one another's arms. The buzzing that was so terrifying outside was threatening to lull me to sleep. Only the pounding heart of my father kept me awake.

Chapter Four

I thought the buzzing was the worst sound in the world. It rattled my bones and sent chills down my spine. It was the constant buzzing that kept my body awake with fear. It was my father whispering almost silently to my mother about our situation -- all of it too soft to make out, but the message of fear and worry was clear -- that kept me alive and awake and full of nervous energy. Even as the night crept forward and threatened to plunge our little village into darkness, I couldn't find the courage to go to sleep. In the end, it was the silence after the buzzing had long gone that threatened to drive us all crazy. I would almost have taken the unending buzzing to fill the deafening silence that followed.

We had long left our corner of distress before the sun gave a hint of sinking below the sky. My mother had prepared a small meal for us earlier, all fruit and vegetables so our fire wouldn't be used. My father had returned to making arrows for the hunters, a new fire in his eyes that made him work faster than he usually would. I didn't go to the loft and sit by myself -- I was still too scared to not have my parents in my sight. Instead, I helped my mother when I thought she needed it. Together we kept busy, cleaning the tidy house to the point of insanity.

It was almost agony, hearing the knock on the door after such a long silence from the outside world. My mother and I jumped, poised to run back to our back corner and hide. My father sprang forward, sharpened arrow in hand. When he opened the door, I didn't recognize who stood there, then again, I don't know many of the Elders in the village. They spoke low, so I was too far away to hear what they were saying. When my father turned away and shut the door, he looked relieved.

"Everything's under control," He began, returning to his seat to continue his arrow making. "The Elders are holding a meeting."

"Isn't it too late for a meeting tonight?" Mother asked, moving to stand by my father. "We should all be asleep to get rest for tomorrow."

"I'd rather this…" He didn't know how to describe what was happening. I wasn't sure I could describe what plague this was either. A message from the gods? An evil twist of fate? How were we to know until the Elders met? "*Thing,*" he settled on, "is taken care of tonight."

My mother nodded, swayed and comforted by his words even though they held nothing but opinions. "Let's just get to bed. We've all had a long day."

"Mila," My father asked, "do you think you can sleep tonight?"

"Not really," I admitted. I tried to look down at my hands, but I wasn't comforted by how I seemed to keep fidgeting, always on the move. I moved my eyes to our one little window, hoping that when the sun finally set, I could see familiar pictures and stories amongst the stars. I was still far too afraid to get any rest now that there was nothing steady to lull me to sleep. Everything seemed foreign and dangerous -- even the painted sky held no comfort for me.

"If you stay up, promise that you won't go outside for anything." He stood up, heading toward the loft where we all slept. "You'll stay in the house tomorrow, but your mother and I will have to hear the verdict of the meeting in the morning. We'll sleep for now, and you can watch out from in here."

My father -- still a Hunter and a Warrior at heart after all this time. I felt honored that he trusted me enough to sleep while I kept watching through the window, but I hardly understood the trust. Maybe Mother had told him about Zolin? Did he think I was so invested in this terrible plague that I'd want to stay up? No matter his thoughts, I decided I'd play his game anyway. Sleep was not an option now, not tonight.

They were slow to climb to the loft. My mother was clearly exhausted, but her eyes still darted around the house as if willing for some imperfection to demand her attention. She hugged me goodnight longer than ever before. My father put a hand on her shoulder, leading her to the ladder. He let her go up first, but before he climbed after her, he sent one pointed look to his creations -- the arrows he had made and the one spear. *He must've finished before I arrived home.* The message he was sending me was clear: if something happens, I am not unguarded.

My father took a long time to climb the ladder, as he always does with his twisted leg. My eyes strayed to the far wall, bouncing between the door and the window. I could see the sky bathed in pink. The sun was definitely setting; the Elders meeting was bound to begin soon. Tomorrow everything would be fixed -- that Thing in the sky, the fear in the faces of the Elders, the preparations of the Warriors. It is all going to be over tomorrow.

We had only one chair in our house. It was normally reserved for my father -- he has too hard a time getting up and down from the mats we normally use -- but I pulled it out of its corner tonight. I sat it in the middle of the house, facing the window. I watched the sun go down, changing from yellow and pink to a deep red. Eventually, the sky turned a dark blue, and finally to the black that we all know well. Slowly my eyes adjusted to the night, and I could see stars beginning to light up the sky. I tried looking for comforting constellations, but I couldn't see anything.

I couldn't stand to sit in the darkness being the only one awake in my house, so I went to one of the shelves and pulled out a candle. I lit it carefully, ensuring that the flame wouldn't be very visible, or visible at all, to anyone out in the village. As I was walking to my chair again, I heard a faint beating of the drums. Five beats in the strong rhythm to mimic the beating heart: *the Elders meeting is about to begin.* I hugged my knees close to my chest, prepared to stay up most of the night.

I had only been in silence for a few moments with my parent's steady breathing for company. My eyes were toward the sky, trying to make out familiar shapes with my limited vision of the stars.

When I heard the quiet knocking at the door, I nearly fell out of my chair. As quickly as I could, I blew out my candle and ran for the back corner of the house. It was cowardly; my father certainly would've jumped for the spear or the arrows, but I wasn't chancing running closer to the window. Thoughts of that Thing filled my mind again, and I sent a silent prayer to the gods. Not now, please.

When the tapping continued, this time taking on a familiar pattern, I realized that I might have jumped to conclusions. When important events happen in the village -- births, deaths, festivals -- Atzi often visits my house late that night. We love to talk about what we've learned or witnessed. I didn't think Atzi would be reckless enough to come to talk tonight, but I still leaped forward when I heard more knocking. Suddenly, there was so much I wanted to discuss, and I threw open the door as quickly and as quietly as I could.

There she was, hair pulled back and clothes unchanged from our earlier work day. I pulled her in quickly, my father's words ringing in my ears: *don't go outside for anything.* We hugged for a while, memories of today running through our heads. When did I see Atzi last? When we were helping the Elders? Surely we couldn't have left each other's minds so quickly.

"The meeting is starting soon," Atzi whispered. We're huddled together on the floor in front of the door now, hiding like criminals from the Warriors.

"What do you think they'll do?" I asked.

"They'll probably say that this is just another mysterious way of the gods." Atzi muttered, "I heard my mother talking to the man who came by to tell us about the meeting. A lot of people think this is a sign."

"Of what?" I asked, "What could we have done?"

"Nothing," Atzi assured me. "We've done absolutely nothing."

"And why are you here? You should be in your house hiding like everyone else."

"I want to know what's going on." Atzi admitted, "Don't you?"

"Yes, but it's dangerous outside."

"Don't you think we have a right to know what's going on? We were there, we saw that monster. Don't you want to know what the Elders have to say?"

"We'll learn tomorrow."

"But we have the chance to learn tonight."

Trying to avoid the obvious was futile. I knew exactly what Atzi was suggesting. She wants to go to the Elders meeting. Elders rarely hold meetings unless something important happens -- planning major funerals or births, wartime efforts, anything that the Chief or the people feel they need guidance in. They always have Warriors surrounding the Meeting House, and meetings usually take place in the day so they can turn curious villagers away. Even though I didn't want to spy on the Elders, I couldn't deny that a plan was already forming in my head. If I could develop a plan only seconds after the idea was put before me, then what kind of plan had Atzi, who has probably been planning this since she heard of the Elders meeting, come up with? This idea was reckless and treasonous considering what had happened today, but could it work?

"It's not allowed." That was all I could think to say. "We'll get caught and we'll be tried by the Chief."

"We'll be tried before the Elders. They won't send out two young, hardworking girls." Atzi reasoned, "I've already thought of this. We say that we were just so worried about that Thing in the sky that we couldn't stay away. We couldn't sleep until we knew what the Chief was going to do about it."

"That's a terrible excuse."

"But it will work because the Warriors aren't used to looking for stragglers in the dark. We'll be quiet and we'll stay out of their line of sight. They won't even see us."

I hardly heard what Atzi said because the beating of the drums had taken up again. Five more beats -- the Elders would be taking their seats in the hall.

"We won't get past the guards," I began, "but if we did, how would we even listen to the meeting? Are you planning on walking through the main door?"

"No. I'll show you when we get there. Are you ready to go?"

I wasn't. I still didn't really trust Atzi's plan. I could see it then, us being thrown before the Chief in the middle of the Elders meeting. We'd be guarded by Warriors for the rest of the night for being suspicious in a time of unrest for the village. If we were lucky, we'd be outcasts for the rest of our lives. If we weren't, we'd be tried before the village. I can't even imagine that.

Even with all of these thoughts in my mind, I couldn't let Atzi go by herself. Together we had a chance, but apart? We'd never have made it this far in our lives without each other. Though my mind was screaming at me to stay inside, I knew I couldn't just let my best friend get into trouble without me. Besides, I couldn't sleep until I knew I was safe. The Chief would tell us we're safe and protected, and then I could sleep peacefully. "Let's go."

It was even more terrifying outside in the night then I had imagined. Every shadow cast because of the moons' light was a hand reaching out to drag us to the underworld. Every mass of darkness became a god threatening to throw us out of the village for treason. Though we stayed low to the ground, I couldn't help but feel as if we'd be spotted by the Warriors or worse. What would happen if the buzzing came back? That Thing would attack the village, taking us all for itself. With all this fear and adrenaline coursing through me, I don't know how I managed to stay silent and on track to the meeting hall. It must have been Atzi leading me slowly that kept me together and quiet.

The Meeting House is in the center of town. It's not tall like the houses we live in, but it's long enough to fit all of the villagers inside if it needed, which it does once a week when we gather to hear the stories of the gods. There are no windows throughout the house, but there is a great hole in the middle of the roof for the fire pit below it. I could see smoke coming out of it now, unafraid of today's events. As we got closer, I could see that the doors to the Meeting House were cracked open. The Warriors that would normally be guarding the Meeting House were preoccupied, trying to listen to the words of the Chief, who I could hear now over the clatter inside. It sounded like he was trying to quiet everyone down. The meeting would begin soon.

We managed to make our way to the side of the Meeting House, where no warrior was waiting. They were so concerned with hearing the meeting that they probably wouldn't go to their posts until they were ordered to, and even then, they'd only be ordered to guard the doors. It was only then that Atzi looked to me and, without making a sound, motioned for me to help her to the roof of the Meeting House. I almost thought she was crazy until I heard the sound of the beating drums once again. This signaled the formal beginning of the meeting, and though I wasn't sure why we were going to the roof yet, I knew this was the perfect time to get up there.

Atzi was on top of the roof by the third beat, and she pulled me up before the fifth one stopped ringing through the air. Then, quickly and quietly, I followed Atzi as she made her way toward the hole in the roof. The smoke was thick and suffocating, but I could see why she was so confident in her plan. We may not have been able to see everything that was going on, but the Chief was almost directly below us, so we could hear everything that he said. No one would concern themselves with the hole in the roof reserved for the smoke to drift through -- they would never notice us as long as we stayed still and silent. How did Atzi figure this one out?

By the time we got in position, the meeting had been called to order. Through the smoke, I could see blurry figures shifting in their seats as they settled for the night ahead of them. The Chief stood at the head of his congregation, eyes forward and vigilant as he scanned the faces of the villagers before him. Someone came to whisper in his ear, and I realized that it was Zolin who approached him. Zolin is only a few years older than me, not even close to being the age necessary to be considered an elder. *What is he doing here?*

He must've brought his father's attention to the Warriors listening at the door because the Chief turned to look at the entrance and ordered the Warriors to get to their posts. Zolin was still too shrouded by the smoke for me to see him well, but the way he marched back to his seat with his head held high had to mean he was showing off. Was this his first Elder's meeting? Why was he here? And why was he sitting away from the Elders, at the front of the Meeting House? Why was he next to where the Chief would sit if someone else were to talk?

The Chief coughed to get the attention of the crowd, "Before we begin, I must ask if everyone is here under honorable and trustworthy intentions."

The words of the gods. The traditions of our people are inspired by the tales of the gods; we mirror their image in an attempt to be as pure as they are. These words, though I've been told and now see that they open the village meetings, originated in the words of the sun god. In older days, some believed our earthly Chief was the sun god reincarnated, but now we're told differently. Now, they are merely the human blood of the sun god -- still important to our survival, but not nearly so holy.

No one says any objections to the Chief's words, and their silence is taken as an agreement to stay honest and trustworthy. The Chief continued, "The horrors of today have terrified our people. Our women and children tremble in their houses, and our men have offered themselves as Warriors in the face of this unknown evil."

I could faintly see several nods from the crowd. I felt Atzi's breathing quicken in all the excitement. We turned to lock eyes, both feeling as if this is a strange dream instead of our reality. Had no one ever really thought of spying on these meetings before? If it's so easy to listen directly to the words of the Elders, why had the other kids not climbed onto the roof of the Meeting House before us? There we were, about to experience firsthand how the Elders governed our village, and no one had noticed us yet!

"We've heard many villagers tell us about this creature." The Chief began slowly pacing in front of the Elders, thinking as he started to speak. "Many call this thing a monster, others a bird sent from the gods. I, myself, am unsure of what this creature could be. I understand many in this room have seen this creature closer than any warrior has. I'm asking you now to come forward and share your experiences with us, so we can better understand what is happening."

The elder women came forward. They all talked about the extreme heat, how working today made us hot, exhausted, and covered in sweat. I felt as if I was living through their stories now, with the heat of the fire so close below me. As I was wiping the sweat off my forehead, I remembered the intense heat of the day, and how we could only cool off by wading in the stream. Then, I remembered the quiet of the animals, and how it felt strange sitting in the forest without being serenaded by birds.

I pulled my focus back to the Elders when they begin describing the Thing to the Meeting House. All at once, I understood why Zolin insisted that I tell him and the other Warriors what I had seen. The women had very poor descriptions of that Thing. The buzzing sound was consistent -- who could ever forget that heart-stopping noise -- but the women couldn't agree on what the Thing looked like. Some called it black, others dark blue, and others green. Half of the women said it was the bird our sun god uses to travel the world, others insisted that it was a creature sent by the god of death. One woman said the thing had feathers, even though I knew I had seen a smooth body.

After they had all told their stories, the Chief held up a hand toward Zolin. Zolin puffed his chest out in pride, and it was obvious now that this was his first village meeting. Why else would he be trying so hard to look confident and strong in front of the Elders? The Chief made room for his son to take the center platform while he took a seat next to where his son had just been. Zolin politely addressed the audience before recounting what he and the other Warriors knew.

"This Bird is darker than a raven and louder than the river after a flood," I remembered my words from earlier today and strained to see and hear as much of Zolin's speech as I could. "The creature moves slower than a turtle, but we didn't get close enough to the Bird to see much."

"Why not?" Someone called from the crowd.

"It turned away," Zolin answered evenly. I was surprised Zolin hadn't gotten angry at the man who openly insulted Zolins' Warriors because, even though Zolin wasn't their true commander, it was obvious to everyone that he was in charge when the Chief wasn't around. "We followed it for as long as we could, but it moved faster when we chased it. We couldn't follow it on foot. Whatever this Thing is, it knew not to let us get near it."

The Chief stood wordlessly, taking his son's place as he let Zolin take his own seat. "You've heard for yourselves what has happened today. I'm asking you all to decide what we should do about this crisis before it gets out of hand."

There was silence for a moment as everyone considered the possibilities. What could they do? There was no guarantee that this Thing would come back, or, at least, everyone was praying to the gods that it never returned. How could they fight it? No one in the village knew anything about it! I moved to see Zolin's face, and the expression he wore scared me. He had his chest puffed out again. *What is he going to do?*

Zolin stood, indicating to the crowd he had an idea. *Sit back down. What are you doing?*

"We should send out Warriors." Zolin announced, "They can see if the Bird is close to the village and lead an attack if they feel threatened. It's the best way to keep the villagers safe."

What?

"If we send out a small group of experienced Warriors, they can track the Bird's path. When they find it, they can destroy it before it has the chance to come back."

"Who agrees with Zolin?" The Chief asked, not even needing to use his influence as Zolin's father to get this proposal agreed upon. "Who thinks we should send out a band of our best Warriors to see that this creature never returns to our village?"

The villagers stomped their feet on the ground to signal their approval.

"And who disagrees with Zolin's proposal?"

The congregation was silent. No one disagreed with the son of the Chief.

"Then tonight we gather our best Warriors. We'll arm them with weapons and supplies. We'll send them in the direction of this creature, and they will make sure it never returns to our village again."

"Come on," Atzi whispered as she nudged my side, "we need to go."

Chapter Five

My parents woke early the next morning to the loud beating of the drum. They kissed my cheek when I kept my eyes closed, tired from last nights unnoticed adventure. This morning, the Chief would alert everyone to what the Elders had decided, about sending out a small group of Warriors to hunt down the mysterious Bird. When my parents left, the sun had still been below the sky, but when they returned, it was now only covered by the trees surrounding the village in every direction. I had woken up to the orange sky not long before they arrived, but had already cleaned myself up, moved my father's chair back to his corner, and started cooking breakfast over the fire.

I wasn't surprised by the grim looks on their faces, but the way their eyes seemed to silently communicate with each other gave me an unsettling feeling. "What did the Chief say?" I asked, playing dumb.

My father shook his head, sitting down heavily in his chair and resuming his work from yesterday. "The Elders decided that they couldn't do anything. It was too dangerous when they didn't know enough about the Bird, as they said it."

What? I thought back to last night, where I remember hearing clear as the sky today that the Chief and Elders planned on sending out a group of Warriors to deal with this crisis. *Surely they hadn't changed their minds since then? How could they change their minds so quickly?* By the time Atzi and I had scrambled down the side of the Meeting House and hid behind a neighboring house, we could see a group of Warriors that had already been chosen. I recognized one of Zolin's friends leading the group.

Where would they have gone if not to search for this Thing, this Bird?

"They're not doing anything?" I asked.

My mother nodded her head, joining me at the fire to help with breakfast. "He's keeping his people's safety in mind. He's also ordered the women to be escorted when we go to the Scavenging Field today."

"Scavenging today? But we scavenged yesterday."

"But it was ended early." My mother explained, "We didn't bring back enough to last us past tomorrow. The Chief ordered us to go to the Field with Warriors to protect us in case the Bird comes back."

I nodded my head. I snuck a peek back at my fathers' corner and noticed that none of his weapons were missing. They hadn't stopped by to get these weapons because they didn't want us to know about the Warriors. *Why?* Why was this a secret they wanted to keep? Were they just trying to save face in the village? But surely people would notice the missing Warriors?

"After you eat, get ready to work." My father said, "We have to make sure this village keeps itself together."

I nodded my head, "Yes, sir."

***

I wanted to walk to the Scavenging Field with Atzi by my side to tell her what my parents had said, but her mother was keeping a very close eye on her. I only had time to say hello before she was whisked away to be brought into a conversation with one of her mother's friends. The look Atzi gave me showed she was in trouble, but for what? Her mother hadn't caught her outside after dark, had she? Did Atzi tell her? Were we both going to get in trouble?

I was so lost in thought that I didn't notice Zolin walk up behind me. I jumped, yelping and catching the attention of some of the women around me. Zolin laughed as if it was perfectly okay to scare me after the creature-incident yesterday, but I couldn't stay mad at him for long.

"Was that your real reaction?" Zolin asked, a grin still on his face. "I didn't mean to scare you so badly."

I shook my head, "It's fine." I noticed the spear in his hands, pointed toward the forest in a constant state of protection. "Is that one of my fathers?"

His smile grew, "Of course. He's the best in the village, I wouldn't use anything less."

Finally, I smiled, "You're too kind."

I thought back to last night, about Zolin announcing that he wanted to send an expedition to go search for the Bird that had come toward our village. They hadn't used my father's weapons, and they hadn't even told him about the warrior's group at all. I know Zolin knew about what really happened to the Warriors, but could he risk telling me? If I asked him, would he try to comfort a good friend by assuring her that everything is being taken care of? Could I ask this of Zolin without making myself look suspicious?

I cleared my throat, "I heard from my parents that the Chief has decided not to do anything about the Bird." I kept my eyes forward, as if acutely aware that I could trip at any moment. "Is that true?"

Zolin took a moment before nodding, "Yes." He leaned closer to me. No one would be able to hear him if he whispered the truth to me now. "Don't worry, everything is under control."

"What do you mean?" I whispered back, trying my hardest not to look at Zolin's face and give myself away.

He shook his head, "I can't tell you. You trust me, though, don't you?

"Of course I do."

He pulled his head away and laughed as if he had only told me a joke. "Good. Don't worry, Mila, I'll keep you safe."

He got that look again -- that prideful smirk lit up his face, and I couldn't help but laugh. "Oh, yes, the mighty Zolin will keep me safe. But I wouldn't want you to show favoritism. That's not exactly allowed, is it?" I chanced a look at the other women around me. I couldn't read any of their expressions.

He shrugged good-naturedly, "Oh well."

I laughed again. "You're going to get me into trouble."

He laughed with me, "I'll get you out of trouble."

"Promise?" I asked.

"Promise."

***

Scavenging wasn't as hard today. The extreme heat from the day before had passed, and we were all still so paranoid about the Bird coming back that we rushed through our work. By midday, we had picked as much as we had done by the end of our work day yesterday. The Elders still weren't satisfied, though, and told us after a small break that we would keep working till sundown if we had to. I complained to Atzi about this, but she said that the Elders probably didn't want to come back here for a few days, just in case the Bird did decide to come back. I didn't argue.

We were sitting by the stream again. We weren't eating as much as we did yesterday, but we also hadn't used as much energy today. It seemed as if Zolin was determined to make us all feel safe and happy and normal because he played with some of the younger children in the shallow parts of the stream. Their laughter was accompanied only by the singing of the birds; the rest of us hardly dared to whisper. When we were working, it was different; the men were standing amongst us and their alert eyes make us feel safe. Now, however, when most of them had decided to doze off while we're all relaxing, we didn't feel as protected.

Atzi and I sat like we did yesterday, close together and away from the other group of women. Atzi's mother tried to get her to sit with her, but she pretended as though she were deaf. I didn't know what was going on between them, but Atzi would let me know if we had been caught, so I didn't bring up their silent feud.

"Did you sleep well?" I asked.

She nodded, "I did."

I couldn't stand her silence. I hadn't seen her like this in a long time. "Now that you've slept on it, what did you think about last night?"

After a moment, she leaned in toward me, "I think something's wrong. Did your parents tell you what he said? The Chief is lying."

"Or he changed his mind," I added hopefully.

She looked at me like I was crazy, "You didn't fall asleep last night?"

"Not with you."

"Then you know he didn't change his mind. It was his son's idea. Don't you notice some of the older Warriors are missing today?"

I looked around and did notice there were some familiar faces missing from the misfit group. It was hard to tell, though, considering I hardly knew the names of most villagers unless they were my age. "They wouldn't send all of them with us anyway. Someone has to protect the village."

She leaned back, finding herself satisfied by my answer, "Why are they all so tired? Were they at the meeting last night?"

I thought back to the Meeting House, to the darkness that seemed to never end. I thought back to the Warriors with their backs to us and their faces toward the main doors, hoping that they could catch a glimpse of what was going on inside. I thought back to the way they hovered around the doors even when they were supposed to be monitoring the sky. They had been so curious about what was happening with the Elders that they gave Atzi and I enough time to sneak away without any of them noticing -- or, at least, that's what Atzi and I thought, seeing as we aren't being tried before the Chief.

"They might have been on guard," I said, "but I doubt they were in the meeting like Zolin was."

Atzi rolled her eyes and turned her head away, "And he shouldn't have been there anyway."

I didn't respond. How could I? No matter what I said, I would be betraying somebody I thought highly of. I nodded slowly, just trying to move our conversation along. My plan didn't work.

"Why was he there?" Atzi spoke with venom in her words as her eyes darted to the boy playing in the water, "He's not an elder. The Chief is in charge of the Warriors, and he only spoke his father's words last night. If the Chief wanted to send a party of Warriors, then he should have said so himself."

Zolin was splashing one of the younger girls with water, but he purposefully missed his aim. He was then attacked by multiple splashes from the girls, nearly soaking him from head to toe. He only laughed, amusing himself as well as the children he was with.

"Is the Chief trying to build Zolin's trust with the Elders?" Atzi continued with no signs of stopping, "What do you think? Why was he there?"

Zolin looked up then like he could sense that we were talking about him. We locked eyes and he smiled at me. I thought he was going to call us over to join him, but he was splashed by the younger girls again and had to retaliate as only a warrior would.

"I don't know." I spoke low and clear, "but, Atzi, I don't want to talk about it." It felt wrong to talk so low of Zolin. I didn't want to do it; he's my friend, and I trust him.

"Why not?" She complained. I had a feeling that if we weren't talking about something we weren't supposed to, her voice would have doubled in volume by now. "He shouldn't have been there. Don't you want to know why he was there?"

"I don't know," I repeated, looking down so I wouldn't have to look at either of them. "I don't really want to know."

***

There was a lot more chatter on the way back to the village. Each woman carried two baskets filled with food, enough to last us a week if we split our spoils well. I walked alongside my mother, watching as she talked with anyone she came across. Atzi was far behind me, walking alongside her mother. After our break, she went back to her mother and I went back to mine. I knew she was mad at me, and I could almost understand why, but even though it's childish, I couldn't bring myself to talk to her. Zolin must've sensed my bad mood, or maybe he was busy entertaining the children when no one else would, because he was leading the group in the front, helping the younger children with their own small but heavy baskets.

The forest didn't look any different to me, but the mood had definitely changed. It was still eerie, with its branches reaching out to grab you at any moment, but now there was more fear to add to the list of terrors this forest had brought me. Even as the women all walked and talked as if it was any summer day, I could see them look over their shoulders from time to time. Everyone was still worried about the Bird in the sky, and they weren't hiding their fear. What would we do if we heard the buzzing again? Would we have to drop everything and run for the village? *What would Zolin and the Warriors do?*

It was a long walk back to the village. When we finally broke into the clearing, it was almost worse than it was in the forest. Everything seemed normal. Men were trading in the village, Elders were teaching the younger girls how to mend clothes, and I could even see the Chief's wife teaching the younger sons stories of the gods with her ecstatic hand movements. The only thing that gave our terror away were the Warriors surrounding the village with their weapons ready to be trained toward the sky, and if you stayed out of sight of the outskirts, you wouldn't even notice them.

We dropped our baskets off down by the river where a separate group of women were already waiting to wash the food we scavenged. I didn't know their names, but I saw they were all more reserved today than usual. They were older -- *could they know something I don't?* I wasn't sure exactly, but they looked to be old enough to have been at the Meeting House last night. Could that explain their quiet faces? As I walked off to wait for my mother to put down her baskets, I noticed one of them fiddle with a small necklace around her neck.

Oh.

Necklaces are given as a sign of betrothal for our people. When a man wants to marry a woman, he prays to the gods and asks for their guidance. He follows in the footsteps of the god of night, giving a hand-carved wooden necklace to the woman with which he wishes to spend the rest of his nights with.

When a man and woman are married, the simple string used for betrothals is replaced by a woven thread the woman makes herself -- it symbolizes the uniting of peoples, and it honors the gods who created the tradition. This woman was married; I could see that now. And she was older, just like the experienced men who went away last night to search for the Bird in the sky.

She was worried about her husband, that much was now painfully clear.

I could see it on the other women's faces now that I knew what I was looking for. They weren't all fiddling with their necklaces, but they had the same misery on their faces. Did this mean the men really did leave last night? I whipped my head around, futilely trying to find the answer with my little knowledge of the villagers themselves. *It could've happened,* I reasoned, *if they were careful enough.* But why would the Chief lie about it? Why would he lie to his people? If we knew the Warriors were gone, these women wouldn't have to work today. They could be in their houses mourning, and we could all be comforting them. Why would the Chief deprive these women of comfort?

I walked back to my house hand in hand with my mother, who refused to let my hand go once she reached me.

"The Chief's son said we should all go back to our homes," my mother whispered. "And we shouldn't leave unless we have to."

I nodded silently, my eyes trained elsewhere. I didn't care if she interpreted my curiosity as fear, I only wanted to see if I could notice if anyone was missing. I needed to know if people were gone. I needed to know if they were truly gone and if the Chief really could lie to his people like I suspected he was doing. And, if he could lie to us now, what had stopped him from lying to us in the past?

"Praise the gods for keeping us safe," my mother muttered. She continued her comforting phrases as we walked through the village, my head whipping back and forth to try and spot older Warriors who could've possibly been the ones sent out after the Bird. "And let them keep us safe for more to come. I don't know what I would've done without you and prayer on my side today, Mila."

It was only then that I saw it. In one of the houses we passed, a woman was seated in front of her door, teaching a group of young girls how to sew. Though the younger girls seemed to be mending some of their own clothes, the woman had taken up another sport. She locked eyes with me as if willing me to look her way. In her hands, sewing for recreation rather than duty, she was sewing a black flower onto her dress. It could mean anything, really, but I couldn't help letting my mind race.

The black flower is the symbol of the god of death. Women use it to praise him so that he may be pleased and keep our Warriors safe. They also use it to mourn the Warriors that have fallen. In some cases, women stand out against decisions they don't agree with by already dawning the black flower, predicting that they will need it in the future.

This was a woman who clearly thought she would need the black flower, and for a mysterious reason, it sent a chill down my spine.

Chapter Six

I knew now without a hint of a doubt that the Warriors are missing. I felt the impulse a few nights ago to ask my father where some of the missing men had gone. I had tried to sound concerned but not curious, just a young girl who had noticed a few missing faces. My father didn't even look up from his meal.

"They sent out some hunters to gather food." He answered, unconcerned, "Just in case we couldn't leave for a while."

I nodded, shocked. *Maybe the Chief has changed his mind...but then why would that woman sew her flower?* "When did they do this?"

"The morning after that Bird came. It was very rushed, but the Chief thought it best to prepare the village in case something should happen."

I nodded, returning to my meal.

It was the next day when I was walking to fetch water by the river with Atzi that I understood what was really going on. Though the group of women was small, it was very noticeable that some of the elder women -- not Elders, really, but women who had been married a long time -- had sewn black flowers that they kept with them. The sight stunned us, and we ran to our spot by the river to collect our water, eager to discuss what we had seen.

"The Chief is a liar," Atzi announced, slightly out of breath.

I shook my head, breathing heavily but still unwilling to announce treason, "We don't know that."

"He sent out those men," Atzi said loudly, pointing her hand in the direction of the village behind me, "and he told the village they were out hunting. We heard him say he was sending Warriors out after that Bird. This is why nobody suspects anything -- he's hiding this from the village!"

"Or maybe they changed their minds after we left," I reasoned, "Why would he lie to his people? The Chief could never--"

Atzi shook her head, silencing me, "They wouldn't reject the golden boy's idea after voting on it."

"Don't call him that."

"Just because you're close to him doesn't mean I have to be blind to his actions."

"I never said you had to be friends with him! I just want you to give him a chance for once."

"You may be willing to overlook his favoritism, but I won't. Mila, don't you see what I see?"

I shook my head, "Atzi, this is treason."

"And what are you going to do about it?" She challenged, "Pray to your stupid gods?"

"That's heresy."

She stormed off toward the river with her pot in hand, and I couldn't even tell if she heard my words or not. She began silently filling her pot with water, making no effort to try and smooth things over with me. With a sigh, I walked to the river, coming to rest beside her. Though she didn't look enthusiastic in the least, she didn't say anything.

"So, do you think the women know their husbands are searching for the Bird, or do you think they're worried that while they're out hunting the Bird will catch them?"

Some of the anger melted from Atzi's face when she heard my question. "I don't know. I guess it depends on how loyal the husband is."

"Or how close the marriage is."

Atzi nodded, "I didn't think of it like that. They could not know at all but just be upset that their husbands are away hunting with this Bird on the loose." She looked thoughtful, letting water flow in and out of her pot as it filled to the brim and filled over, "I wonder if I can ask around and see."

My eyes widened, "No, you can't!"

"Without giving us away." Atzi corrected, "Obviously."

***

Because I had little to do for the rest of the day and my mother was concerning herself with staying busy, she allowed me to wander the village in order to help some of the elder women with their own work. I tried to focus on the women with their husbands on the mysterious hunting trip, as most of them had children that were already living on their own, and they had to take care of themselves. I was just taking a pot from one of the women to fill with water by the river when I saw Zolin not too far away. He was with Necalli; it looked like he was teaching him how to shoot arrows properly. After everything that had happened since I last saw the younger brother, I had forgotten about his terrible aim.

I didn't mean to stare, but I got distracted by their relaxed air. Just having Zolin next to him made Necalli shoot straighter, and every arrow he shot landed inside the tree he was aiming for. Zolin was a supportive brother, cheering Necalli on with every arrow that left the string. The boys joked with each other, laughing and smiling as Necalli ran toward the tree to collect his arrows. Zolin looked up then, meeting my gaze. I tried to look away before he noticed me, but I'd already been spotted. Though he didn't have to, Zolin ran up to greet me.

"Hey, Mila." He said, eyes bright with energy, "What are you doing out here?"

"Getting water for some of the women in the village," I answered, motioning to the pot I held on my hip.

"That's kind of you."

I shrugged, "It's the least I could do," A thought occurred to me, "since their husbands are out hunting."

Zolin looked toward the river, but that didn't mean he was hiding something. He could've just been scouting the land. That was something Warriors did, "You've always been helpful."

"I've noticed some of them have been wearing black flowers." *He can't hide this from me for much longer, can he?* "Do they really have so much to worry about?"

Zolin looked from me to the river to his brother, who had gathered all his arrows and was watching us intently. Zolin seemed to be thinking to himself before he shouted to Necalli, "Keep practicing! I'll be back!"

"Are you walking me to the river? You don't have to do that."

His eyes never left the ground in front of him, "Come on, Mila. We're friends. I want to." He waited till we had walked down the river a little bit before he got closer to me. *Is this it? Will he tell me now?* "Are you worried?"

"About what?" I asked, suddenly wishing I had never pried. *He isn't going to tell me.*

"About this Bird. About what it means for us." Zolin didn't look at ease; he didn't want to have this conversation but must have felt he needed to. I could see in his expression he was desperate to talk about anything else, but the way his hands curled into fists showed he knew he needed to push on. *What is he thinking?*

"Of course I'm worried," I answered, trying my hardest to sound like a village girl who only knew what her parents had told her. *Pick your words carefully, Mila.* "We still don't know if this Bird is going to come back."

Zolin nodded. "Is that all you're worried about?"

I didn't like the way he was looking at me. Why did he have to look like he knew everything? "I'm worried about the hunters," I admitted carefully.

"They're experienced," Zolin answered.

"But we don't know what we're dealing with. We don't know if this Bird is good or evil. We don't even know if it is from the gods or not. It could be anything." *Take the chance,* "And I don't think sending out Warriors is the best idea when we don't know if they could come back."

"Hunters."

What did I do? "What?"

"Hunters." Zolin corrected. "You said Warriors instead of hunters."

Oh no. "Oh, yeah." I looked down, hoping my face wasn't turning red.

Zolin got quiet for a moment. By then, we were just walking beside the river, not stopping to fill up the pot even though we could at any point. We were nearing mine and Atzi's spot. *I need to stop this before it gets any worse.*

"Mila," Zolin said, "you don't need to worry." He spoke slower now, carefully. Just to give myself something to do, I jumped ahead and began filling the pot I had with water. "Everything is being taken care of."

Please fill faster, I commanded silently.

"You know," he hesitated, "I was at the Meeting House two nights ago. I was sitting with the Elders."

No, you were sitting in front of them. "You were?" I kept my face to the river. My heart was beating fast.

I could hear Zolin pacing behind me. "My father said it was important that I learn how the village runs. He has big plans for me." He paused, "I was so nervous, I had to focus on the fire in front of me to calm down."

Dear gods. "I didn't think you were ever nervous." My attempt at a joke didn't seem to sit well. Maybe it was the tightening of my throat that made my words sound all wrong. "Did everything go well?" *Is he looking at me? Gods above, don't let him look at me. Don't let him know.*

"I watched faces in the smoke appear and disappear to keep me focused. It was better than looking at the Elders tell different stories over and over again when they hardly got the facts right."

He knows. He has to.

"I thought you would've been taking in every detail. It's your dream to be Chief, isn't it?" Does my voice sound normal enough? Can he sense my fear? Isn't he one of the best hunters this village has seen? Does he know?

Zolin moves to sit beside me, turning to look at my expression which threatened to reveal me. He moved as if to grab my hand or my wrist, but he couldn't quite decide on which one. He ended up grabbing some sort of in between, and I couldn't tell if the gesture was supposed to comfort or intimidate me.

"Mila, you--"

In all my fear and fast heartbeats, I forgot what I was doing. The water pushed the pot out of my trembling hands, threatening to carry it down the river. Zolin acted fast, catching the pot hardly after it left my hands. I knew I seemed guilty now, but I was shaking so badly that I hardly cared.

"I'm sorry," I say, breathing deeply to try and steady myself. "I wasn't paying attention."

"You're fine. Are you okay? Mila?"

I shook my head, grabbing the now half-filled pot from Zolin's hands. "I'm fine, I promise." I couldn't even convince myself. "We should head back to the village." A thought occurred to me, "I don't like being so far away with that Bird around."

He seemed unsure. It was like he wanted to ask me about my reaction but couldn't bring himself to do it. *Please, Zolin.* I begged in my head, *Please.*

In the end, he caved, standing up beside me with a weak smile on his face. "Let's go."

We spent much of the walk back in silence, both staring at the ground in front of us so we didn't have to look at each other. *Zolin knows I'm worried, but does he know what I'm worried about?* I couldn't decide if he was naturally curious or trying to get me to confess. Would he tell the Chief? Or had he known for a while, and wanted me to own up to it before he told? Would he keep my secret? Could I ask him, or would that give me away?

By the time we got back to the outskirts of the village, I had stopped shaking. I held the pot of water close to my chest, using it to try and shield me from the rest of the world. Zolin took the hint, leaving space between us, unlike the last time we had walked on this trail. It was only when we could hear Necalli's arrows piercing the tree that he spoke again.

"Mila," He paused, but I couldn't understand what the momentary silence meant, "everything is going to be okay."

I nodded and kept my eyes to the ground. I couldn't bring myself to look at him, either. *What if he sees through me?*

He sighed, "Take care." He put a hand on my shoulder, willing me to match his gaze. Willing me to give myself up. I couldn't. He moved quickly, looking down as he ran back toward his brother. I stared after him for only a moment before heading back toward the village, eager to get back home and away from the boy who may or may not be able to accuse me of treason.

***

I was sitting alone in my home, willing the sun to dip behind the earth so I could pretend to sleep. That moment was still forever away, but that hadn't stopped me yet from trying to force the sun to disappear. My father was out in the village, delivering some of his weapons to the Chief to be distributed. My mother was visiting some of the Elders, helping them with various chores that needed to be completed before nightfall. They left me alone, however wary. My mother even offered to take me with her if I wanted. Not wanting to risk running into Zolin again, I decided to decline.

It Came from the Sky

I sat on the edge of the loft that held our mats above the floor, sitting next to the ladder so my legs could swing back and forth freely. My eyes had been glued to the window since I got home, but that hadn't changed the sun's speed in the slightest. When my arms started hurting from holding my body up, I laid on my back, only catching glimpses of shadows as the sun moved down the sky. It wasn't an ideal position -- and it certainly wasn't very productive -- but it was all I could muster.

Does he know? It's a chorus that was echoing through my head. *Did I ruin it all, or did he already know? Was he giving me a chance, or was he thinking about something else? Did he know?* I sighed, tired of myself asking questions that I couldn't find the answer to. I couldn't call my emotions heartbreaking; the word didn't sit right in my mind. *What is wrong with me? What's the matter with you, Mila?*

I pushed myself off of the loft, not even bothering to use the ladder as my parents would've. I paced my house for a sense of action and purpose but came up empty-handed. My mother kept herself busy today, leaving nothing for me to keep myself busy with. *Almost.* I could see in my father's corner where he had been working in a hurry, as a mess of shaved wood and small pieces of rocks were visible. *That'll work.* I stooped down to the floor, eager to do something meaningless so I wouldn't have to think about today at all.

At first, I was so lost in thought that I didn't notice anything was wrong. The village was noisy tonight, finally awake from its frightful slumber. I heard bartering and trading outside, as well as the laughter of the children at play. Somewhere, someone was teaching a child the words to a song -- something festive to be sung to the river god at our next festival. *They'll need all the time they can to practice.* I tried to focus my mind on the unsure singing.

Even when I noticed something was wrong, I chose to ignore it. *It's all in my head.* I assured myself. When that didn't work, I told myself: *it's just the river.* My eyes kept darting to the window, willing the sun to sink further and my mother to come home. *It's all in my head. It's just in my head. Keep cleaning.* But there was nothing left to clean anymore, and I could no longer avoid the obvious. The people in the village had gotten quiet, too quiet, and not even the sound of birdsong could pierce the air.

The Bird was back.

This time, it was closer; it had to be. It was the only explanation for the shaking of my house. All the little pieces I had been holding went crashing to the floor, and I couldn't help the scream that left my lips. I couldn't even hear my own panic; the buzzing was so loud. It seemed to be shaking me; shaking my village; shaking my world. I could feel it deep in my chest, but I knew this pulsing was not the pounding of my heart. This was the Bird, the creature, the Thing, come to kill us all.

The walls were shaking so much that things started flying off of the few shelves we had up. I screamed again, diving under the loft to cover myself from any flying objects, grabbing onto the ladder for some sort of support. Pots shattered as they hit the dirt floor, and knives stuck in the hardened, worn down mud. I covered my ears and closed my eyes, willing everything to disappear. *Please, please, please.*

All at once it stopped. Had the sky opened up and swallowed the Bird whole? I was too busy crying with my hands shaking over my covered ears to process anything. I heard screaming from people who were just as terrified as I was. Without thinking, I bolted for the door, praying that my parents would be outside waiting for me. They have to be. I couldn't be alone.

I saw chaos. The villagers that were so peaceful outside had lost all thought of what they should do. I saw women and children running into each other in their haste to get to their homes. Men were running everywhere, trying to decide where they should go -- to their weapons or to their families. I saw some men run towards others with weapons in their hands, yelling out orders that I couldn't really hear. They ran to the edge of the village, where we thought the Bird was going to come from the last time it appeared. Was that where it came from? Was that where it went?

"Mila!" My mother slammed into me before I even saw her. We were both crying, and she pulled me into a tight embrace. "We need to get inside."

"Where's--"

"Get inside!" My father's voice boomed, and I saw him coming toward us as fast as he could. He looked as if he was in pain, and for a second, I wondered if he was moving too fast for his hurt leg to handle. My mother started pulling me inside. Her hands were tight around me, ensuring that this time I could not be pulled away by anyone.

"Call the Elders!" A voice yelled from somewhere in the village. It was a voice so strangled with fear that I couldn't even recognize it.

Chapter Seven

If knowing the Bird is above me was bad, then having to stay inside for hours waiting for the Bird to come back is worse. The Elders were ready for their meeting, but the Chief refused to begin until he was sure everyone was safe. He went personally from door to door with a small group of Warriors, checking in on everybody and assuring them that the Bird was gone. My father was sitting in his chair, face glued to our single window. My mother paced by the door. I sat on the ground by my father's side, my hands seemingly stuck forever in his. We weren't crying anymore, but we were all still shaking as if we'd never stop.

The light knock on our door nearly caused us all to scream again. We jumped, and my mother rushed to open the door as quickly as possible. She tried to usher the group of Warriors inside quickly, but frowned not soon after. My father stood up then, just as confused as me. My mother heard something neither of us could hear before she stepped aside, letting Zolin come through our door.

"We need to speak with the Chief. Outside." My mother said, sending a quick look my direction. I understood, now, why the Chief felt he needed to be guarded by Warriors. They didn't want to scare the children. *They're taking parents outside, leaving the children to sit in the safety of their homes.*

Zolin closed the door behind my father, seeming impatient for him to leave. The moment he could, he ran toward me and came to sit beside me. He put his hands on my shoulders and made me face him.

He spoke low but quick, "Are you all right?"

"Are you?" I asked, "Is Necalli?"

"We're fine." He assured me, "You were inside? You're not hurt?"

"Of course." I said, "What are they saying out there?"

He didn't hesitate to answer, "The meeting will take place after the sun sets, so we have time to gather the Elders and make sure everyone is safe."

"Why are they afraid to say this in front of me?" I asked.

Zolin shook his head, "It's just custom, I think. That's what I've been told."

I nodded my head slowly. "Are you going to this meeting, too?"

Zolin looked pained, but I couldn't understand why. Was he regretting telling me his secret? There was no way they could hear us from outside. Could this even be a secret if all of the Elders know about it? "Yes."

"What will they do now?" I asked. *What can they do now?*

Zolin doesn't have an answer for me. He pulled me toward him in a quick hug that made me feel neither comforted nor reassured. "Everything is going to be fine."

"Stay safe," I whispered back.

The door opened and Zolin stood up quickly, not wanting to embarrass either of us in front of my parents. He left without another word to me, letting my parents enter the house before he left and closing the door behind him. My parents, oblivious to my knowledge of their conversation, filled me in on what they knew.

"They're calling another meeting." My father announced, walking slowly back to his chair, "It will start after the sun sets."

"They have to do something now." My mother said solemnly, "They say the village is terrified."

"They should be praying. We have nothing to fear," My father said angrily. "This is just what I said was going to happen."

"What?" I asked, shocked.

"Mila, this village is not what it used to be." My father began, "The children don't want to pray and the men don't want to worship. I knew the wrath of the gods would rain down on us, and nobody listened to me. No one listens to the stories of the gods anymore, and now we've made them all angry."

"We shouldn't scare her," my mother interrupted, but my father didn't listen.

"She should know the truth." It's so quiet in my house. "Mila, this Bird is a plague that is going to divide our village into the believers and the frauds. They will not disrespect our gods anymore. The gods will have their revenge."

It was too silent after his speech. I had never heard my father talk this way. I didn't know how to respond.

***

We all pretended to go to sleep early, but, unlike my parents, I purposefully stayed awake long after sleep first called to me. I waited for the beating of the drums and then the slight knocking on my door before I moved, checking to make sure my parents were asleep before I descended the ladder. I knew Atzi would come tonight. Why wouldn't she? She was just as interested as I was to know how the Chief would fix this problem. *Will he continue lying, or will he come clean to the village? What will his new plan be?*

It wasn't as easy this time, sneaking toward the Meeting House. The Warriors were now less interested in the meeting and more interested in their actual jobs following this second sighting of the Bird. By the time we managed to sneak around a particularly interested shadow of a Warrior and pull ourselves on top of the Meeting House, the meeting had already begun. The beating of the drums managed to cover our movement, and the Chief's words, filling the Meeting House like a sermon, surely drowned out any scurrying we made to the hole in the roof.

"Yes, the Bird has come back," he said this as if we all hadn't witnessed this scene a few hours ago. "My heart is heavy with what this news means."

Atzi nudged my arm, face grim. I looked at her curiously, trying to understand the cryptic message. She mouthed two words to me: *the Warriors*. They're not coming home.

"But," the Chief pulled me out of my thoughts, "we cannot let this tragedy consume us. We still have a village to protect. In time, we will mourn, but not tonight."

Why not? I asked silently, *isn't that what we're supposed to do? Mourn for the Warriors that won't come home?*

There was a commotion among the Elders, but I don't think it was because they agreed with me. They were riled up like the Hunters before a hunt. This was the most energy they'd had since the Bird arrived. They were ready to make decisions; they were ready to follow their Chief. *But what will he do? What will they decide now?*

In all the uproar, I searched for Zolin. He was in the same seat as the last meeting, but tonight he didn't look as smug. He was still sitting up straight -- as confident and strong as ever -- but the emotion on his face is what worried me. His mouth seemed to be set in a permanent frown; his eyes look dazed. It was as if he wasn't paying attention to the Chief at all. He reminded me of when I'm tired and don't want to scavenge or go to the weekly gatherings for worship -- this is the look of desperately wanting to be anywhere besides where you are at that moment.

"Tonight," the Chief once again pulled my attention back, "we fight back against this monster, for taking our Warriors and forcing our people to cower in fear!"

The uproar was so loud, I wondered if any of the villagers could hear it. I didn't even have time to hang on to what the Chief had said before he pointed at his son and called him up to stand beside him. It may have just been the smoke, but Zolin looked green. Were his hands shaking? It was hard to tell, especially when he turned his back to me. For comfort, I grabbed Atzi's hand. She seemed just as lifeless as Zolin.

"The last group of Warriors had orders to watch before attacking. They needed to decide if this Bird was a threat to our people." Zolin says, "We now know that this Bird is more dangerous than we thought. Our next group will be different. Offensive from the beginning, we will destroy this Bird before it even sees us." He sounds so confident, and the applause of the Elders surely helps. Why, then, does he seem more like a child now then he has since I've known him?

"My son," the Chief interrupted, a hand on Zolin's shoulder, "will personally lead this next band of Warriors! With his guidance, we will free the village from torment!"

And the crowd goes wild.

It was just like when Zolin or one of the other boys won a game at a festival. Everyone cheers regardless of which team they were supposed to be cheering for. The Elders stood up, stomping the ground or pounding their fists in the air. They began to chant a warrior's call. The Chief raised Zolin's fist in the air, and it really did feel as if all of this is just a sick game. My heart felt like it had stopped beating. It was as if I watched him get injured right when he went for a goal. My breathing was erratic as I tried to calm myself down. Atzi's grip on my hand tightened, but I didn't dare take my eyes away from the father and son standing below me.

In all the commotion, Zolin returned to his seat. As he sat, his eyes turned to the fire pit, no, to the rising smoke. It was as if he was looking right at me, telling me with his eyes that I shouldn't have come. I could hear his words in my head: *now you see. This is why you shouldn't be here, but now you know the truth.* I was stunned. I felt as if there were holes burning into my skin from the way he was looking directly at me. *He must know I'm here -- this can't be a coincidental glare.* But then, just as I thought he would call to me, he looked away.

His eyes didn't leave the ground for the rest of the meeting.

***

With every sunrise and sunset, I prayed to the gods, something I hadn't done since I was a child. I prayed for the safety of the Warriors, for the ones who haven't been seen or heard from in the days following the meeting. Everything feels too tense and so, so wrong. Atzi, desperate to get us both out of our homes, had asked me to meet her in our spot at midday. Though I hated leaving the comfort and safety of my parents, I agreed anyway.

When I got there, Atzi was already sitting with her feet in the river. Her eyes were closed, but I knew she sensed I was there when she lay her back against the rock and huffed in agitation. I went to join her but left my feet out of the water.

"They aren't back yet," I said.

"None of them are." Atzi agrees.

"Why would they send out more Warriors if the last ones aren't even back yet?"

Atzi gave me a look I seem to receive frequently, "Do you remember the way they talked at the meeting?" I nodded slowly and she continued, "I don't think they are coming back."

"How could they know that?" I inhaled shakily. *They could be lost -- we don't know. They have to come back, don't they? They have to.*

Atzi shrugs, "I don't know, but that's how they sounded."

I pulled my knees to my chest, "Does the village really believe the Chief sent out more hunters?"

"No one questions anything the Chief says," Atzi stated matter-of-factly. "And anyone who does can be charged with treason for all he cares."

"Atzi," I warned.

"It's true," she defended. "Why do you think all the flowers the women were wearing have suddenly disappeared? The Chief probably ordered them to stop."

Have they? "Why would the Chief do that? It doesn't make any sense."

"Well, he probably doesn't want his wife to get involved," Atzi said bitterly, "because she probably would have."

I didn't have anything to say about Etapalli. What could I say? No one had seen her since the last time the Bird came, or, at least, that's what Atzi told me. I heard the same of Necalli, the poor boy who looked up to his brother as if he were one of the gods. I'd seen the Chief every day since the Bird came, trying to lift the spirits of the villagers. I always had a hard time looking at him.

"The Elders have changed since the meeting." I said quickly, "They don't look nearly so confident."

That much is also very true. If I wasn't a villager here, I would almost think the Elders at the meeting and the Elders now were different people. Though they smiled at the women who were missing husbands and sons, they looked otherwise completely defeated. There were no smiles or confident nods to other Elders. Everyone looked so lost. It was as if they thought the son of the Chief could solve their problems before the sun rose, but only now were they worried that they made a terrible mistake. Now, they had risked making the same mistake twice with the same outcome. And why? What could they possibly gain from killing this Bird with a secret group of Warriors?

"It serves them right," Atzi said suddenly, "for sending out Warriors before they even knew what they were dealing with."

"We still don't even know now." I agreed.

"Exactly." Atzi nodded, "They're sending out these Warriors to die and they're only now feeling sorry about it. I bet it's only because Zolin's leading the charge. They're worried they just killed a future Chief."

"Atzi," I couldn't take her rivalry today.

"Sorry."

"What do you think they're going to do?" I asked, trying to redirect the conversation.

"The Elders?" Atzi asked, "Nothing. They can't do anything without revealing themselves."

"What if they send a new group of Warriors to search for the fake hunters?"

"Another group of Warriors? That's the problem they should be avoiding."

"Would you be surprised if they did it anyway?"

She didn't have a response for me this time.

Chapter Eight

"You're not hungry?" My mother asked, looking toward my plate that was still full of food.

"Not really," I pushed my food away. "Can I go to bed?"

My parents looked at each other, and, even though I knew they were worried, I couldn't bring myself to feel guilty. I hadn't eaten since breakfast, since before I talked to Atzi down by the river. I haven't really had the appetite since. We sat there for what felt like hours trying to predict what the Elders would do. We both hope they all come clean to the village, but Atzi can't help but have a feeling that they would never do that. I don't entirely disagree, either. Every day, it seems the Chief is urging us to pray more often and the village is listening -- they value his opinion too much to disobey. The Chief won't want to give up that kind of power by admitting he sacrificed two groups of Warriors -- his own son, even -- for something the village didn't know about, didn't vote on, or even agree to.

Thinking of the Warriors makes my eyes drop to the floor. I can hardly bring myself to think of them out of fear for their safety. *What did they think when they were told to go after the Bird? Were they afraid? Did they try to resist?* I wish I knew.

"If you're not feeling well, then you can be done." My father said mercifully.

"Thank you," I put what I didn't eat back into the large bowls in front of me. I climbed to the loft, confident that neither of my parents would disrupt me for a while. I lay on my mat facing the ceiling, and even though I didn't want to eavesdrop on my parent's conversation, I couldn't help it.

"She's been like that since she came back," my mother said. I couldn't see her, but the worry was evident in her voice. "She said she went to meet with Atzi by the river."

"Then you shouldn't have let her go," my father said. I could hear him eat as he continued scolding my mother, "I can only imagine the nonsense that she's filling Mila's head with."

"I wouldn't say that," my mother argued. "They have fun together."

"That child is just like her father. She has a brain for trouble. Before we know it, she'll be dragging Mila down with her. Hasn't she already? Weren't they late to the Fields once?"

"That was a while ago." My mother said sweetly, "And she's still a kid. We weren't perfect when we were her age."

"I was never late for work."

"You followed the strict schedule of the hunters." She argued.

"And I was committed."

"Very. I'm not saying that's a bad thing."

"No, it's a good thing." My father was stern. I'd never heard him speak of Atzi this way. Thinking back, I've never heard him speak of anyone that way.

It was as if all the years of Atzi and I taking care of each other didn't exist. I knew where his hatred stemmed from; he used to be friends with Atzi's father, but that still doesn't seem like a good reason to dislike Atzi so much. It was a surprising revelation, to learn how deep the anger had taken root. *How have I never heard this before?*

My mother sighed, "If something bad happens, you can blame me, but until then, I don't see a problem with her."

My father huffed, "Fine."

They were quiet now, each one of them trying to finish their plates in an annoyed silence that I hadn't witnessed in a long time. I rolled over on my side, attempting to shut out their anger. It wasn't working very well, because then I had nothing to do but think, and I really didn't want to do that. I could only think about Atzi's words and, what hurt the most: Zolin.

How could the Chief send out his own son? It was like a war raging in my head, except I was only a witness and had no say in who lives or dies. Zolin is strong and smart, yes, but he's hardly older than I am. If strong, experienced Warriors don't come back after dealing with this Bird, then how could he risk Zolin, his choice for future Chief? It made no sense, and yet that's what has happened.

Atzi told me on our way back to the village that the Chief was just seeking honor and glory. *For him and Zolin,* she had said, *like he's always done.* I refused to believe her, remembering all the good, noble things Zolin had done for the village. Atzi was as persistent and unwavering as ever. It was only when she hinted that it might've been Zolin's ambition driving the plot forward that I drew the line. *How could she say something like that about one of my closest friends?* I had said goodbye abruptly, and I didn't turn around until I was in the safety of my own home.

Even now, I refused to believe Zolin could be behind this in any way. Did Atzi not see the fear in his eyes at the meeting, or did she not care? I had never seen Zolin shake so badly in my entire life. In fact, I'd never seen him shake at all. He was afraid; that much anyone could see. So why, then, did the Chief still send him out into the forest? Why had

Zolin's mother or brother let him leave? Could they not say something to make him stay? Why would they agree to send out more people to die?

Just try to sleep, Mila. I told myself, knowing that I was far too worked up now. Sleep seemed like an impossibility, especially since, if I couldn't focus on my parents, the Chief, or Zolin, my mind automatically drifted to the Bird. It hadn't been seen for a few days, and many villagers seemed to be trying to bring their daily lives back to their regular routine. How they could all still say they felt safe at a time like this was beyond me. Gods or no gods, every time we managed to feel safe, this Thing came back and brought fear and pain back into our lives.

Just thinking of the Bird made me feel paranoid. *This time the Bird will stay away,* I reasoned in my head. *It has too.* Can something really bring such continual terror? Can we really be haunted by this Bird until the end of time? No, I refused to believe it. I couldn't believe it. Because, even though I fought with Atzi and distrust the Chief, I could not help but feel as if everything would somehow turn out alright. It had too. This would not be a story I tell my children so they will believe the gods. This was the reality; this was the truth. Bad things couldn't happen here, where it is the village pulling the strings instead of the Almighty.

My paranoia seemed to be growing the more I thought about this Bird. Every crack of the fire below me reminded me of the unstoppable buzzing. It was so silent in my house, much too quiet for my mind to be at ease. I turned over on my mat, putting my back against the floor of the loft. *Why are my parents being so quiet?* At least with their arguing, I wouldn't have to imagine false sounds in the night to frighten me.

My eyes flew open from where they had been closed only moments before. I was so still I think I forgot how to breathe. Everything was so quiet, too still to possibly conceive. I suddenly felt as if I was alone in the whole world. Had my parents left me here, or had they forgotten how to breathe too? The fire flickering against the walls sent shivers down my spine and filled my mind with thoughts of monsters. *You're scaring yourself,* I tried to reason. I was willing to try anything now. *Everything is going to be fine.*

It wasn't quiet in my house anymore.

The buzzing wasn't in my imagination.

The Bird was back.

Without thinking, I lunged for the ladder and begin climbing down to be with my parents. I don't know if it was the fear of being closer to the Bird or my wish for someone to hold me like a child, but I felt as if I was flying down the rungs to reach my parents in only a heartbeat. It was my mother who grabbed me, pulling me close to her chest as if ready to face anything that might come through our door. My father grabbed a spear that wasn't quite finished, but aimed it at the door anyway -- ready to fight whatever he must.

The buzzing was immensely loud, louder than it had ever been before. I should have been frightened, I should have been scared beyond my wildest nightmares. I couldn't even bring myself to shake. It was as if I had gone numb, and not even my mother's shaking body beside me could snap life into me. I thought of the Warriors, the ones who had been sent out and called dead by more than one person. *Is this what the Bird is doing? Taunting us?*

I heard a scream from another house. Someone was outside when the Bird came, and the fear was spilling from their voice in an agony that would make the river freeze over. "Look," they yelled, as if begging the world to see what's before us, "it's back!"

It's that close?

It was the familiar voice of a woman, but I didn't know who it belonged to. I heard another scream, one that must have sent fear into the hearts of every villager. I saw the outside world darken out of my window. *What's happening? Where did the moon go? What's happened to the sky?* I don't think -- I just act.

I dashed from my mother's arms. She tried to reach for me, but I was already out the door, searching desperately for the source of the scream I heard. I couldn't even see the woman because of the absolute darkness outside. My eyes were unable to adjust to the sudden change of lighting. There was nothing helping me see the world around me. The moon really was gone. My mouth dropped open, an involuntary action I couldn't stop. *Someone has hidden the stars.* No, not someone. The *Bird.*

I could see its silhouette against the black sky, creating an even deeper blackness that brought a chill down my spine. I saw the outline of the Bird now, but its shape hardly reminds me of a bird. It was large, seemingly able to take up the clear sky the village once owned. Though I could see the body and wings of a bird in the shape, it didn't seem as if the Bird was really alive. How could it be when it didn't even flap its wings?

The buzzing was so loud that I stumbled back, feeling its power deep in my chest. The Bird moved slowly, inching across the sky in an act that both made the buzzing louder and the sight of the slowly absorbed stars more petrifying. More screams fill the air. The whole village must've followed me outside. I didn't know when my screaming joined the chorus of panic, but I recognized the soreness of my throat long before I was able to regain control of myself.

I think we all expected the Bird to fall from the sky, landing on us and crushing us all. When that didn't happen and the stars slowly began to reappear, we all fell silent. I could see clearly the path of the Bird now. Its persistent route had taken itself right over us, but still at the same steady pace it always had. It was only moving over us, passing over top of the village. *What is it doing? Watching us? Waiting to kill us all?*

My father finally grabbed my arm, yanking me behind him in some defensive gesture. I'm sure he wanted to yell at me, but he was just as stunned as the rest of us by this extraordinary sight. The Bird, in all of its terrifying glory, was passing right over us. I faintly heard the beating of the drums and the call of the Warriors. They were gathering to defend us now, but by the time they did so, the Bird would be gone.

In that instance, I was entirely right. The Bird was nearly gone before I even saw any Warriors run past us in the direction the Bird was facing. My father left my side at some point to join the commotion of men desperate to help in some way, but my eyes stayed fixed to the sky. *It's just leaving.*

It's flying away. No one could do anything about it, and the Bird was flying away as it had come.

My mother tried to grab my arm, "Let's get inside."

She pulled me back as my eyes stayed transfixed to the sky. We both stopped, however, when the most heart-wrenching sob reached our ears. We looked over, and I was horrified to see Etapalli and Necalli standing nearby. I don't know why they were so close to us -- maybe their family had run out to usher everybody inside -- but I understand what she must be feeling. *Zolin...*

The pain that hit me was intense, but it couldn't be half as much as what the wife of the Chief felt. Necalli caught her before she could fall and make a scene in front of the other villagers. With his back toward me, he began ushering his mother toward their own house, all while yelling at people to get indoors to safety. For a brief moment, I thought Etapalli was looking toward me, trying to convey some message through her eyes, but I only felt as if I was going crazy, just like she seemed to be.

"Mila," my mother snapped me out of my reverie. She pulled me again back toward the house, but this time I didn't have the strength to resist her. I was too consumed with thoughts about the wife of the Chief. *She thinks Zolin is dead.*

Chapter Nine

Another meeting was called so late into the night that by the time the drums began, my parents had already resigned themselves to a restless sleep.

"You can stay up if you want," my mother said tiredly, not even trying to sound like her usual self. "Use candles. Put out the fire."

"I will," I assured her. We hugged as if we would never see each other again before she slowly ascends the ladder. At that moment, she didn't look as if she'd slept in a while. I hardly got a moment to worry about her before my father called for me to extinguish the fire. I grabbed a candle and lit it before pouring water into the fire pit. The flames departed with a sickening hiss, bathing the house in an eerie glow provided by my single candle.

I went to sit in my father's chair, not even bothering to move it to the center of the room. I already knew what was going to happen tonight: Atzi would want me to spy on the meeting with her. Despite my earlier actions, this time I was determined to turn her down. I didn't think I could stomach another meeting. Could I really sit back and watch the Elders send off more people to die? I felt l as if I was in mourning, but how could I mourn for someone who is only assumed to be dead? In my heart, I hoped the Warriors were still alive, but my mind told me otherwise, and I knew my eyes would be unable to prevent tears if I had to see another person break down the way the Chief's wife did.

The knock at my door hardly surprised me. I made sure my parents hadn't stirred and waited for their steady breathing to reassure me before I set my candle down on the ground beside me. Creeping to the door felt too familiar, and I didn't like it. Atzi came in quickly before I hardly had the chance to open the door. She listened for the quiet breathing of my parents before she started talking.

"The meeting will start soon. Let's go."

"No." I whispered back, "Not tonight."

"Why not?" She seemed so undisturbed; for the first time in my life, I found myself wondering if she's completely sane.

"If people really are dying," I managed to choke out, "then I don't want to be a part of it."

"So Zolin disappears and you give up?" Atzi was not the type of person to beat around the bush. No, Atzi jumps for the throat. "Wouldn't he want you to, I don't know, honor him by exposing the Elders?"

"To who, the people? The Elders run the village, Atzi, they'll be forgiven."

"Well, I'm already here. Just come with me this last time. I won't come back like this if you don't want to see any more meetings."

Her eyes were narrowed and her mouth set in a thin line. I could already see a future where she doesn't forgive me for turning her down -- that's how Atzi is bound to react. Could I really lose her over this? I shook my head, wishing more than anything that I had just gone to sleep like my parents.

"This isn't a game anymore, Atzi. We know people who are missing. This is real."

"It's always been real. Just one more night," she promised me. "I'll fill you in on any more meetings."

I felt like crying, but my eyes were dry. "Promise?"

"Promise."

The drums would be beating soon. *This is the path of least resistance,* I told myself. *And maybe I owe this to Zolin. He would want the village to know the truth, wouldn't he?*

"Let's go."

'

***

The meeting started with angry yelling and stomping feet. The Elders were beyond worried, that much was clear. They were being so loud, I wondered at first if they wanted the entire village to hear them and figure out what they had done. But what good would that do? Their sound rose and fell based on if various revelations came to their attention or not, but almost always there was a constant stream of noise that, at it's worse, sent vibrations through the air that I felt hit my chest. It felt like the Bird was coming back again, except this time I would feel no sense of fear or worry. The Bird couldn't hurt me now; it probably wouldn't be back for another few days. I grabbed Atzi's hand to steady myself from the chaos below. This meeting seemed to be unlike any other.

The Chief was struggling to call order to the Elders. He tried yelling, he tried commanding, he tried banging a spear on the ground to sound like a drum. Nothing worked. After a while, he settled for silence, reminding me of his wife when all of the children were too worked up to focus on the gods and their boring stories. His arms were crossed and his face stern. He did not tap his foot, but considering the state he seemed to be in, this came as a surprise. The Chief didn't speak a word or move a muscle until the Elders had calmed themselves down. It was only when they resume the orderly quiet and obedience they usually exert that the Chief began the meeting properly.

"Before we begin, I must ask if everyone is here under honorable and trustworthy intentions." I thought the Elders would go mad again with their yelling and their stomping. How many days ago did they praise the Chief and clap his family on the back? What made them decide now was the best time to turn on their beloved leader? For once, I was thankful that the Elders were so rowdy because it took a few moments to get my bearings on the situation before me.

"Now that everyone has said their piece," the Chief began, setting off a chorus of mutters that only ended when the Warriors banged their spears on the ground in support of their commander, "we must come up with a plan of action."

"No more hiding in the dark!" One man yelled. It was still hard to see through the smoke from the fire below us, so his face remained masked. His voice, like many of the Elders, was unfamiliar to me.

"And what do you suggest we do?" The Chief asked calmly.

"This is his domain," Atzi whispered to me, eyes locked on the scene before her. "Watch carefully."

"It was all of you who agreed to send out the first group of Warriors. It was one of you who came up with the idea to keep this knowledge safe from the rest of the villagers." So, that's what happened. The Elders were murmuring now, taken aback by the blunt honesty of their leader. I had never seen the Chief look so accusing. He was changed, "You all demanded that we send out more Warriors to recover the bodies of the first. Not even a day to mourn our fallen!"

The Warriors in the Meeting House, a sight I now realized I had never seen before, hit their spears on the ground again to show respect for their fallen, as they typically would do in ceremonies and festivals -- not Elders meetings. I looked at Atzi with worry written all over my face, but she didn't even notice me. How could she? The very heart of the village seemed to be collapsing before our eyes, and we were helpless.

"So, I ask you now not as your Chief, but as a fellow villager in mourning," Atzi scoffed beside me, "what do you suggest we do?"

There was an unsettling silence coming from the Elders now. Did they really not have a plan? Are the Elders typically so useless? I felt like Atzi suddenly, as if she'd been rubbing off on me while we were spying and adventuring. How many times had this Bird come to us, and how many times had these Elders met? Had they really just been willing to go along with whatever Zolin said no matter what? Yes, he was a good warrior and the son of the Chief, but was that all they look for in a leader? No substance? No honor? Is this how the village was truly run?

In all my thinking, I realized I missed a suggestion from a man toward the front of the congregation that I can just barely see. It was too late to understand what he said, but the reactions of the Elders were split on the issue. The Chief managed to quiet everybody down, but he looked different.

"I understand your want for prayer, but now is not a time for custom and grace. Now is the time for action. Prayer is not the answer to all of our problems right now."

The Chief's answer stunned us all -- from Atzi to the Warriors standing at attention -- into silence. The Chief, telling us that prayer won't help us? It's blasphemy, heresy. Had my mother been in this Meeting House, she would've fainted for fear that the gods would strike us all down now. The Elders seemed to be shocked into silence, a first as far as I was concerned. They couldn't scream and yell; unable to even bang their feet on the ground in protest.

"This is a test from the gods." The Chief announced. "We are being tested by the very beings who have created us, and we're failing them. How many more tests are we willing to fail? How far will we push the very gods who create and love us? The mighty sun god, patron of the Warriors, is sending us a sign of contempt and anger. Are we willing to answer the call with purpose, or will we confine ourselves to the wrath of the gods?"

"Are you saying we're cursed?" A woman in the front asked. It was so silent that, even in her almost-whisper, her voice carried throughout the Meeting House. It seemed as if the Chief felt no shame whatsoever in saying such a thing. He lowered his head, looking as if he were praying. When he raised his head, though I couldn't see his face, I knew he must look frightening. Many people toward the front of the meeting leaned away from him. What else could draw such looks from these people whose whole lives were spent convincing the village that they were fearless?

"What else could explain the events we've seen. Warriors are disappearing, probably dying, on our orders. The men we've sent to protect us aren't coming home. This hasn't happened before. We must have angered the gods. We're not in their favor anymore."

This caused the outrage the Chief was lacking earlier. Many Elders stood in protest, begging for their yelling voice to be heard over the others. Atzi and I stared at the scene before us -- we'd never seen a riot like this before. Some Elders moved as if to talk to the Chief personally, but were deterred from such a decision by the Warriors, who had moved in between the Chief and the Elders in a defensive stance. The Elders seemed even more upset with this action, as more of them took to their feet now to try and give their grievances to the Chief. The Warriors had yet to point their spears at the Elders, but at this rate, I couldn't see how much longer they'd hold off before declaring the Elders as a danger.

Suddenly, almost out of nowhere in the chaos, a voice rises above the others. "I know what to do! I can stop this! I know what to do!" The crowd of angry Elders eventually calmed down enough to listen to the words of this man that I could not see. Several Elders turned around, trying to find the voice that promised to have all the answers. The Chief himself took a few steps back from his vantage point a few steps above the Elders, trying to see the voice that claims to have the solutions eluding even the Chief.

The voice still continued, and with some maneuvering, I managed to faintly see a man standing toward the middle of the crowd. He had a stick with him acting as a cane, and his hair was pulled back in a way that showed he was one of the caretakers of the Meeting House. When we held services for the gods, much like we're scheduled to soon, he would be in charge of making sure everyone is both at the Meeting House and worshiping properly. The gleam in his eyes reminded me of the times when I was scolded for not bending low enough for prayer or not moving enough when dancing. I didn't know who this man really is, but I didn't like him.

"You have an idea?" The Chief asked this as if this man had just raised his hand instead of interrupting a small riot. "Come forward. Speak."

The man, though he looked small and frail, didn't take long before he reached the Chief. He bowed low, a symbol of both praise and respect. Even though the fire pit was below me, I still felt cold. I didn't like the way this man looked at the Chief when he thought no one could see him. *He's hungry for something.* His face was still unrecognizable to me, but the way he stood reminded me of Zolin at his first meeting. *He's prideful. He has nothing to lose and everything to gain.* I don't trust this man.

"I have prayed to the gods," the man announced himself not to the Chief, but to the Elders. "They show me a way we can end our fear."

"How so?" A woman's voice called from the crowd.

"There is only one way to appease the gods and regain their favor." He paused for dramatic effect before he whispered the one word that chilled my blood and stops my heart from beating, "sacrifice."

I hoped the Elders would riot again, maybe band together to throw this man out of the meeting. But everyone was silent. They were all thinking, not of how crazy this man looked and sounded, but about how maybe his idea -- the first they had heard since the idea for Warriors to kill the Bird -- could work. This quiet, this silent thoughtfulness, made me shiver. *Surely they can't be thinking this will work?* Our gods are peaceful, why would they call for blood?

"Explain." The Chief commanded, but he didn't even sound appalled, just curious.

"Atzi," I whispered, "I think we should go."

"In a moment." She responded quickly. She was curious too. She wanted to hear what this man had to say. My heart sank.

The man paced before the Elders like he had done this his entire life. "The Warriors we've sent out are dead, there is no doubt of that. Why haven't they returned yet if they're supposed to be tracking the Bird? This Bird has shown up to the village and those brave Warriors haven't. They have surely left his world." There was a slight sniffle from among the Elders, and the man gave a good pause before he continued again. *This is all so fake, so staged. Is any of this even real?*

"The only thing the gods are getting out of our terror is the blood of our fallen. That is the only thing they receive by scaring us into hiding in our homes. This cycle of fear is still happening, so the gods must want more blood."

"But they're getting blood." One warrior pointed out.

"Unceremoniously." The man paused again. I wished I could see his face; see what he was doing to win the favor of the Elders. "I see your faces and hear your chants when we spend a day in festivals. If your tired, uninterested actions offend me, then how do you think the gods feel? They see you moving your mouth but not shouting in praise. They see you look around to humor each other while we're supposed to be in prayer. This village has been dishonoring the gods for too long, and now they want their revenge."

"With a sacrifice?" The same warrior asked, "But we don't do that anymore."

I could see the man nod as if he hadn't thought of this before. Judging by how quickly he responded, however, he was only humoring the boy. "Our last great Chief declared the ceremony cruel and unnecessary, yes. But that was after a time of faithfulness and tribute. We are nothing like the last Chief's people. If we could see him now, we would see his shaking head and disappointed face. We have angered the gods. We have angered our ancestors. To return to their favor, we must honor them as they would have honored our spirits before we descended upon this world!"

It was once again like a rowdy sporting event in the Meeting House. Elders loudly yelled their approval. The Chief seemed to agree with his silence. There was the thumping of canes and the stamping of feet on the floor. If what I witnessed earlier was a riot, this is a revolution. The Elders were not only happy to comply with the cruel wishes of this man who says he speaks for his gods, the Elders were eager to serve. My stomach felt sick. It seemed as if the heat from the fire had warmed me too much, and I was threatening to faint and fall right into the fire.

"Atzi, please," I whispered quickly, tearing my eyes from the sight before me to look at her unreadable face. "I want to go home."

Her eyes didn't leave the meeting for a moment, and I was worried that I would be forced to make the trek back to my house alone. I could already see myself getting lost in the shadows trying to navigate my way home from this Meeting House of nightmares. When Atzi finally looked up at me with a softness in her eyes, I felt as if I breathed for the first time since this man stood up and raised his voice.

Atzi nodded at me, "Let's leave while they're too worked up to notice us."

We were moving across the roof now, not even having to try to conceal our movements with the loud cheering coming from below us. "Can we really let this happen? Are they really going to kill someone for the gods? Are we even sure this Bird comes from the gods?"

Atzi didn't look at me. Instead, her eyes turned to the stars and the familiar patterns we knew so well. She shook her head. "We'll get your father. He has some influence with the Chief; my mother said they used to be close when they were both hunters with my father. Maybe he can talk some sense into the Chief. Maybe if the Chief sees how unpopular this idea is, he won't let it happen."

Though I thought any influence my father used to have with the Chief was surely long gone, I decided to not let this worry me. My father would fix this. He could save the poor soul in this village who will lose their life to the new-found insanity of the Elders. He could stop this madness.

"We'll have to explain everything," I said quietly. "We'll have to tell him about the other meetings and the missing Warriors." Atzi nodded, silently thinking over what I said. I wondered if he would be angry with us, blaming us for the trouble we'd overheard. No. My father would fix this. He loves me. He would help me. *And if the Chief turns on him?* Unthinkable.

Before we jumped down from the roof, Atzi got my attention with her hand on my arm. "Don't think about it now," she advised. "Just focus on getting home. We can't risk running into a warrior tonight."

I nodded my head but didn't say a word. How could I possibly not think about what I'd witnessed? The memories of the meeting consumed me, and I didn't have the energy to push those thoughts away.

Chapter Ten

This was our first attempt at sneaking home while a meeting was still going on, and even though the early escape still seemed absolutely necessary, I couldn't help but feel as if it was a terrible idea. The cheers of the Elders inside could still be heard very clearly from our position next to the Meeting House, which only helped create the mood outside into one of terror. Every time the yelling surged, I had the increased impulse to look behind me for a warrior jumping out to grab us. I had the unending urge to look to the sky, but I wasn't even sure what I feared anymore. We stood by the side of the Meeting House longer than we probably should have, but it seemed like neither of us wanted to be the first to move.

"Come on," Atzi whispered. She led me as she always does, taking my hand and dragging me along behind her. I let her do all the work of searching for patrolling Warriors and timing our moves. While she took me home, I let my mind go over everything I just witnessed. It kept me occupied and less likely to break down into a crying, shivering mess.

They're planning a murder. It was the truth I could not speak yet knew was absolutely true. My father, when I was younger, always told me stories about the Chief that protected the village when he was a boy. His name was Chief Elan, and he was one of the greatest Chief's my father ever bothered to tell me about. My mother says Chief Elan was my father's idol, and that was why he never had a bad word to say about him. *He was only a child for most of the time that he guarded us,* my mother would say, *he can't really remember these silly things about the Chief.*

My father would swear there wasn't a rainy day if Chief Elan didn't pray for it. If the village didn't take care and head his words, then the scavengers and hunters would come back with nothing. Chief Elan promised to weed out the disobeyers and punish them, not with violence, but with love. He outlawed the sacrifices that haven't been mentioned since tonight. He, like many others who were too afraid to speak out, saw only harm in the practice. Animals were one thing, but people were an entirely different matter. My father praised him as a man of vision and triumph. I've never met another person who spoke of him so flawlessly.

So why, then, would the Chief try to undo his father's legacy? My father said the village celebrated for days when the sacrifices were outlawed. They made a chair of vines and flowers and lifted Chief Elan high above their heads. Etapalli loved to tell stories about her father-in-law, declaring him the best Chief the village ever had, second only to her husband. Why would the Chief agree to destroy what his father had worked hard to make sure would never be undone? Why bring back the sacrifices, and without even thinking of how the villagers would react?

He can't think the village will agree with him, I reasoned in my mind. I chanced a quick sprint with Atzi in between some houses, not even focused enough to look in the direction of the supposed warrior. Atzi may have been battling with clueless Warriors in her effort to get us home, but I was having a war of a very different kind. This is a war against everything I've ever believed in, and I had a growing suspicion that I was losing.

Will they agree because of the Bird? Will the village be angry because of the dead Warriors? Can they still trust a Chief who lied to them? The child inside my heart said yes. The Chief was there to lead us through the difficult times, and wasn't this just another difficult time through which he would take us? Shouldn't we trust him with our lives, as he was honor-bound by the gods to protect us? Yet, in my mind, I knew what my answer would be. *Can I trust a Chief who has lied to me?* No.

What did this even mean? We dodged another warrior by ducking behind the opposite side of a house. Atzi paused momentarily to catch her breath. I watched her breathe deeply in concentration and calculation. What would she say if she could hear me thinking? I'd always known she never really trusted the Chief -- she doesn't really trust anyone, in my opinion -- but what would she think of my treasonous thoughts now? Would she congratulate me on seeing the light? I didn't know what to think about anyone anymore.

"Mila," Atzi whispered softly, "stop dancing around in your head."

I snapped myself out of my daze, though I didn't do it out of love for my friend. "What do you think will happen to us if we tell my father what we've been doing?"

Atzi had the decency to not look too annoyed, but I knew now was not a time for questions. "We can figure out when we get to your house."

I chanced a look around us, "No one is here, Atzi, and I think I'm going crazy. Please."

"What do you want me to do? I don't know what's going on either! This is exactly what I've been worrying about since I was a child. We are nothing to the people around us, and I don't even know if anyone will believe us."

We were both hostile, but we quickly snapped out of our annoyance with the world. There was the sound of a twig breaking in the distance. "What was that?"

Atzi didn't risk another word. Her grip tightened on my arm as she pulled me along, weaving between homes as if she were a deer escaping a hunter. Our breathing was heavy, and I was afraid we would lead any pursuer right toward us in our haste. Atzi threw me down behind some large pots holding fruit and joined me there. We were out of breath and trembling. All thoughts of sacrifice ran from my mind when I heard the footsteps were still close to us. *What do we do?*

"Who's there?" A young voice called. I didn't recognize it immediately, but it sounded familiar. This was not an older man whom I forget the name of for lack of interaction. This was someone I must know. The male voice is confident but small. He was on edge, but eager to discover us. I could tell by the way his shadow kept. "More men are on their way. Come out now."

Atzi shook her head silently at me like I was really considering handing myself over to this boy of a warrior. Through the cracks between the boxes we hide behind, I saw the shadow of a man. Though his face was bathed in moonlight, I still could not make out who he was with. I could only see his confident stance and feel the terror slide over me. He was young, but definitely one of Zolin's Warriors. He looked strong and he was clearly fast. Could we make it past him? I saw the mischievous gleam in Atzi's eyes. She had a plan.

She grabbed a small rock by her feet. In a moment, I understood. This could work. In the darkness, I hardly saw her throw the rock away from us and toward a stack of boxes. The sound it made was faint, but just enough to throw suspicion away from our location. I wanted to congratulate Atzi right there for being a genius, but I held my breath. And I'm glad I did because only a second later, four more Warriors appeared behind the other one. Though I couldn't see their weapons, they looked intimidating enough.

"I heard a sound." The first warrior said. I was confused why he seemed to be leading them when their shadows gave away he was more than a head shorter than them all. At this point, he whispered something quietly, faintly motioning to the spot where Atzi threw her rock. When she saw this, Atzi pointed to my right, where we had a clean stretch to dart off and disappear before the Warriors even noticed. My house wasn't too far away; I felt as if I could already see the faint glow of the candle I left behind. Adrenaline coursed through me.

The four Warriors disappeared into the darkness they came from, and I thought they were going to try and corner the rock Atzi had thrown. I couldn't help the smile that spread across my face. *Zolin would be proud of me.*

"You need to show yourself." The boy warrior demanded, inching slowly toward the other boxes. In one of his hands, I saw a spear pointed in the direction he was walking. He looked tensed for action, but not as if he was trying to frighten us. "No villagers are supposed to be out after dark."

I heard the faintest of rustles from the darkness and knew the four Warriors must be preparing to attack their rock. This time, I was the one to grab Atzi's hand in preparation for the sprint. As focused and alive as I felt now, I knew that nothing could stop me from running home and waking my father. He would fix everything. He would stop the Chief from making a decision without consulting the village. I almost felt a thrill come over me. Would they tell stories of me someday? A story about the girls that stopped the sacrifices?

"We have to turn you into the Chief," The boy continued, "but don't be afraid. We won't hurt you."

You won't even see us, I gloated in my head. I was tensed, saving our escape for the exact moment the Warriors would pounce on thin air. *Any moment now, five Warriors will feel like fools as two girls evade their capture.* My heart is pumped fast with the tension of waiting.

I could see the boy warrior prepare to give his signal. His hand was raised, and the minute it came down, I would bolt for my house. We would make it home before the Warriors can figure out where we really were. *Focus, Mila.* I told myself. *Watch him carefully.*

His hand lowered. My feet threw me forward like a bird taking off for the air. For a moment, it felt as though I was flying. Only a moment. I slammed into something hard. It felt like a tree; a tree that grabbed me with arms so tight I know I had no hope of escape.

Atzi was ripped from me. We kicked and screamed for each other. Two hands grab one of my arms and two hands grab my other arm as Atzi and I were pulled into the open by the four Warriors. All the air seemed to disappear from my lungs when I saw the boy warrior I thought I was outsmarting. There stood Necalli in a way that mirrored Zolin so much that I felt tears rising in my throat. If I wasn't so terrified, I might've screamed.

"To the Meeting House." Necalli ordered. I didn't even have the heart to look at Atzi, who was still kicking and fighting as if her life depended on it. *But it might.* The sick thought left a hollow feeling in my stomach. I didn't think I had the energy to fight anymore.

We were forcefully marched to the Meeting House. Though Atzi and I struggled, I knew it was useless. The Warriors had strong grips, out of which it was impossible to break. We were pushed side by side with the Warriors, and Necalli was leading the charge. He stood with his back straight and his head held high. When he turned us in, he would be a hero not only to his father but to the Elders. He would be keeping the peace in the village. Did he know what this might cost me or Atzi? Did he know what is really going on?

"Necalli," I tried to reason with him. We were nearing the Meeting House. I was sure the Warriors standing guard could already see us coming. "you can't turn us in. They could call this treason. You know what that punishment is -- they could kill us!"

I thought I saw him shaking his head, but I couldn't really tell. "We need to turn you into the Chief." He said simply. "You will be punished, but you won't be killed."

"Do you even know what they're saying in there?" I asked desperately. "They're going to--"

"It's none of my business to know." Necalli interrupted me. We had arrived at the door now, and I didn't think there would be any more reasoning with him.

"Listen, kid," Atzi started, but the Warriors holding her pushed her roughly to get her quiet. Fearful with a sense of helplessness, we watched as Necalli whispered something unintelligible to the warrior guarding the door. The warrior looked to the others for only a moment before ordering them to surround our group. They were too busy worrying we'd run away to see us trembling. Atzi and I locked eyes, but we didn't dare say anything to each other. *What could we say?*

It was Necalli who finally pushed open the doors and led us inside. Atzi and I were brought in and then thrown to the ground. Our arms are forced behind our backs as our knees hit the ground, catching us before we fell down completely. I didn't have the heart to look up and meet the curious gazes of the Elders before us. I focused my attention on Necalli's feet and my unsteady breathing.

"What are you doing?" The Chief asked sternly. I watched as he came into the edge of my vision. He was moving to stand in front of his son. "Why do you have these girls with you?"

"I found them out after dark." Necalli proudly announced. "They were running away from the Meeting House. I think they were spying on you. They said they knew what you were saying." There were a few gasps from the Elders. I felt the heat rise in my face. *We we're doomed.*

"Is this true?" The Chief directed his question towards us. When neither of us responded, one of the Warriors behind me pulled on my hair, forcing me to look the Chief in the eyes. I was pained by how much he resembled his eldest son. "Answer me, child." His warning fell on deaf ears. Atzi and I shared an unspoken pact of silence.

"We caught them near the Storage House." Necalli continued, "I warned them that they had to come before my father for being out after sunset."

The Chief began to pace. I felt my breathing steady as I saw more and more of Zolin in this man. *He won't let us die, he just can't.* Zolin was my friend -- he must know that. Surely he wouldn't kill someone who was close to his son? Surely he wouldn't hurt the daughter of an old friend? The Chief was here to protect the villagers, not destroy them. *I'll be fine,* I thought to myself. *We'll be fine.*

"Do you have anything to say for yourselves?" The Chief finally asked. The pain at the back of my head begged me to respond, but I remained silent. When the sound of a man standing amongst the crowd of Elders reached my ears, I couldn't stop my eyes from widening or my breathing from speeding up. *Not him.*

"Might I suggest a solution to both of our problems?" It was the voice from before, the man who spoke out earlier. *No.* Seeing his face up close sent shivers down my spine. He was older, his face adorned with wrinkles that make him look ancient. His eyes were darker than the night sky, making him appear more like a spiritual, malicious force of evil than a man. He looked just as twisted as my mind had imagined while I was running away with Atzi. His mouth seemed to be set permanently in a sinister smirk. My heart sank.

"What are you saying?" The Chief asked. His eyes darted between Atzi and me, but I couldn't read the emotions hidden in his brow. I could only register that he was speaking as if he already knew what was coming next, and I think that was the worst of it all.

"To regain the favor of the gods," the old man said, "we need to appease them with blood. I believe two holy lambs have just been escorted into the Meeting House. Two lambs that know things that cannot leave this place."

I only wished now that the Bird would show its ugly face. Why couldn't it show up now, at the moment I needed it most? I wished that unholy buzzing would pierce through the air, throwing the village into another panic so I could run home to my parents. I just wanted to see my parents.

"You're asking me to kill children?" Why was I still unable to read the expression behind the Chief's eyes?

"I'm asking you to send them to their true home -- the palace of the gods -- as a holy sacrifice to save our village."

Now the tears came easily, flowing down my face with no sense of grace, dignity, or honor. Now, I felt hopeless.

"No!" Atzi yelled beside me, "You can't! You can't kill us! You can't kill us without approval from the village! You can't keep sending children out to die without letting the village know! You--"

"Send her out." The Chief doesn't yell. In fact, I hardly heard him myself. I watched as Atzi was dragged from the Meeting House kicking and screaming.

"Murderer!" She yelled with such a passion for life in her voice. I'd be surprised if the entire village wasn't awake now. "Murderers! You're all murderers!" Her voice was choked with emotion. I turned away. *I can't watch this.*

The tears flowed so quickly now that my vision was blurry. I felt as if I couldn't breathe, and seeing Atzi crying as she was dragged away has made this entire experience far too real for me. What was going to happen to me? What was the Chief going to do? I did the only thing I could think of.

"You betrayed your son!" I screamed with all my heart and lungs. I screamed what I know to be the truth. "You are no Chief! You are no leader! You are a wolf in sheep's clothing! You will kill us like you killed your son!"

"Send her away." The Chief yelled this time. I found a sad joy in the painful shock on Necalli's face.

I did not agree with going out quietly.

"You murdered those Warriors, you murdered your son, and now you will murder us! You're a liar! You sent your son to die, and now you send me to join him! Murderer!" The sobs that racked my chest were painful, but I didn't let them silence me.

"Murder! Liar!"

I was out of the Meeting House now, under the night sky.

"You killed your son! Just help us! Please help us!"

I couldn't scream anymore. My voice was hoarse and my spirit broken.

Now I could only whisper, "I don't want to leave. Take me back."

My sobbing didn't convince the Warriors to turn around.

Chapter Eleven

The Chief declared it a kindness that he let us be confined in our homes, but this doesn't save us from death and he refused to let us see our parents. I only knew this news because I could hear the whispers of the villagers outside the single window of my house. There were many Warriors outside my dwelling to stop my contact with the village, but no one could stop the sounds that came through my window. Once or twice, I heard what sounded like sobbing, and I wonder if might be my mother standing outside. What did she think of me? Had the village learned anything about my situation? I couldn't say for sure.

The entire village gathered in the Meeting House the morning after we were restrained. I could hear some of the fiery sermon from my house -- that's how passionate the village was. I heard Atzi and I condemned as treasonous snakes. We were to be sacrificed to the gods "for the safety of the village". These were the necessary steps that must be taken for peace and prosperity to return to the villagers again. I heard nothing about the missing Warriors. I didn't think the village would ever really know what was happening right in front of them. The only good news out of this treachery was Necalli's new status as a hero to the village. I heard that, after the festival, he would be given medals and status; surely, he would be the choice for next Chief. He would never be as good as Zolin would have been.

An older warrior brought me some food and water. He didn't look me in the eyes when he saw me, and he hurried so as to spend as little time as possible in my presence. Whenever I saw him, I wondered how Atzi was doing. I hadn't seen her since she was dragged away. Did she have to see the look in her mother's eyes when they told her what we did? I remembered clearly the tears that streamed down my face as I was thrown in front of my parents. They tried to help me at first. They were shocked when they heard my fate, but they didn't dare argue with the orders of the Chief. I thought they would fight for me. They walked out the door without looking at me.

It was when I was finally getting accustomed my solitude that the Chief decided to honor me with his presence. It was midday, and though I'd managed to fall into a quick sleep a few times since my imprisonment, I was still achingly tired. I sat in my father's chair, which I had moved to the center of the room just for the occasion. My hands were bound by rope, but my feet were left free. If I really wanted, I could move around; make a scene; scare the villagers witless. But I felt too defeated to leave that kind of mark on my home. I hadn't moved since the Warriors threw me down, tied me up, and threatened me with their spears if I even tried to leave my house.

Seeing the Chief in his ceremonial outfit made me want to scream, but I stayed silent. That's what Atzi would do, isn't it? She wouldn't talk to him unless she was tearing him down. She never liked the Chief, and now I wish I had listened to her when I could. I still hated seeing how much he looked like Zolin. Instead of looking into his face, I decided to focus on the spot where Zolin last spoke to me. He was worried then, I'm confident now that he already knew his fate. He was saying goodbye to me. Did he know that he would see me later at the meeting? I guess I can ask him when I see him.

"Hello, Mila." His voice was calm, considering the last time we spoke to each other, or, rather, considering the last time I spoke to him. Instead of replying, I thought instead back to last night. Though I was still kicking myself for getting caught by Necalli, it felt good to get everything off of my chest, even if it was just insults aimed at a man I used to respect. I felt lighter today. I had lifted a weight of emotions that were no longer holding me down. If I wasn't confined to the house, I might have dared to say that I felt free.

"I'm assuming you'll be much like your friend. She was silent -- like you -- until she decided to tell me exactly what she thought of me."

He had prepared for me to be uncooperative; he looked like he was also preparing to stand for a while. He had a giant stick with him acting as a cane, and though I'd never seen him use it before, he leaned on it as if it was his only support. I wondered if this was a new accessory or just another lie he had been hiding from the village.

"It's fine if you're silent." The Chief assured me, "I have a lot of talking to do."

Gods, if you're real, I began, but I thought better of it. It seemed all this time I'd been doubting Atzi when she has been right. Why not believe her about the gods too? What had they done for me, except perhaps sentence me to an early death? No, there was no mystical force to help me. I needed to face this on my own.

"The comments you made last night were hurtful but honest. I can see that you really believe everything you've told me. I can hardly blame you.

You're not the only person who's expressed those opinions."

Etapalli or Necalli?

"I only wish you had expressed your fears more privately. We wouldn't be in this situation if you had."

Liar.

"Your friend told me that you two began spying on the meetings after the first appearance of the Bird. Is this true?"

Silence. He seemed to take it in stride.

"That's what I thought. I understand why you did it, of course. You two were worried about your people and your family. If I were you, I might have even done the same thing. Without getting caught, of course."

I closed my eyes so he might not see how much hate I held for him. I don't think my plan worked well. He continued, seeming more like a man telling a story than a Chief talking to a criminal.

"It's a shame that things have turned out this way. There was a time when I saw a very different future for you. Your father would agree; we're both very disappointed in you."

Don't talk about my father.

"But, even now, I don't really blame you. I'm here to help you."

I laughed, a sound that was both rough and joyous to my ears. *Help me?* I could no longer comprehend a world where the Chief wasn't a liar. My pride wanted me to laugh him out of my house, but I held myself back. I hadn't gotten the chance to hear everything he had to say, and I was curious to find out why he had been here monologuing to me instead of leading his people.

"Mila, you're a kind girl. Zolin would--" I couldn't tell if his voice cracked or if he was afraid to say the words. His pause was abrupt and short, and just intriguing enough that I looked up at him for the first time, "say good things about you. He thought highly of you. I know you don't believe me, but I don't want things to end this way."

"Why did you send him to the Bird?" I couldn't stop the words from leaving my mouth.

Before I left this house, I would know why -- I had to know why.

He paused for a moment before speaking, "He was strong and brave. He was an obvious leader. I loved my son; I didn't think he would die."

"Why are you trying to save me now if you couldn't even save him?"

"This is for my conscience, child." The Chief was losing patience with me now. "I know what I've done, and I accept my consequences, good and bad. There are too many children dying, and I'm trying to fix that."

"What about Atzi?" I asked quickly, "Are you saving her, too?"

"She's her father's daughter. They're both troublemakers that few people in this village trust. It wouldn't be hard to convince them that you were just following her evil ideas and plans. We can pass the blame onto her -- it's the only way to convince the Elders that you're innocent and the only way to save you from your fate."

"Which is?"

"It will be decided tonight how the sacrifice will go. It's up to the Elders."

"Why would I ever believe you? Or," I raised my voice now, "why would I betray the one person in this village who tells me the truth?"

"To survive." He said simply. "You won't see your parents again if you don't denounce the child as a traitor."

He couldn't possibly expect me to betray my friend, could he? I wanted to see my parents again, but how could I face them knowing I lied to save myself? How could I face them with the knowledge that I let my best friend die? I could not compromise my morals for this man -- I had already given him too much.

"How does it feel?" I asked. I had made my choice. "How does it feel being such a disappointment to your father's legacy?"

Of all the jabs I'd thrown toward the Chief, this one seemed to hit the hardest. Maybe it was the one he was least expecting, or maybe this is something else entirely. I could see any chance of mercy previously offered to me flying away faster than the mysterious Bird.

"You talk about things you don't understand." Suddenly, the Chief looked more like a Chief. His back grew straighter, he had stopped leaning on his cane, and his face was the blank mask the village had grown accustomed too. This was a man willing to do whatever it took, no matter the cost. "I will not ask you again. Will you denounce your friend as a traitor for your life?"

"I have honor. I have pride." I struggled to find the right words. He had already turned away, anticipating my answer. "I have loyalty."

"Then I can only pray that the Elders take pity on you both. Your fate is out of my hands."

It was only after he left me in the silent, empty house that the long forgotten tears started to flow freely again. I forgot the air of mystery I concocted for myself. I cried.

No one bothered me until nightfall. Not even the warrior who was supposed to bring me food risked interrupting me at a time like this. I didn't care if I seemed like a child; I didn't care what the world thought of me. I realized that this could be my last night to see the stars, and here I am, crying like a newborn over things I can no longer control. I tried to clear my mind and think of nothing, but that only made me think of the things I was trying the most to avoid. Each moment was agony for my heart, and the burden I had been so sure I could carry only weighed me down more as the sun left the sky.

Even though I believed I made the right choice, I couldn't help but wonder if I shouldn't have taken Atzi's side. She was my friend, my closest friend, but I spent my time thinking seriously if she was worth dying over. *She's a troublemaker. I'm not. I don't want this to happen to me.* Then I remembered all the times we spent together growing up. I thought of our spot by the river, of our bickering in the Scavenging Fields, of all the times when she teased me for trying to be in favor with the Chief's family. This was a girl, as hurtful as she could be sometimes, that would never betray me. I thought of how proud my parents would be if they knew how honorable I was. *They would be proud of me, wouldn't they?*

Night officially arrived. Still, no one had come to see me or, most importantly, bring me any food. I had long stopped my crying in the hopes that the Warriors would not be afraid of a girl under control, and yet they still didn't feed me. *Is it almost time?* I risked sneaking glances from my window, but I saw and heard nothing. The Warriors were keeping watch faithfully, and the villagers were all sound asleep. I was alone for the night. Despite warming thoughts of honor and loyalty, I felt so completely alone in my dark house. I tried not to think of my parents but failed spectacularly. Even when I began to succeed, I only thought about Atzi or Zolin or the unknown path ahead of me.

There was a brief moment of commotion outside that startled me. I heard whispering too quiet for me to make out, and I saw only the dark silhouette of a warrior moving. *What are they doing?* I tried to look outside, but it was too dark for me to see anything. A stark silence fell, followed immediately afterward by a low mumbling. Someone didn't want to be overheard. I was afraid to risk running to the window, but curious as to what's happening outside my house. The warrior I could see through the window turned to look at somebody, and though I couldn't really see his expression, I could tell that his spear isn't raised. Whoever was outside, they were somebody I surely know. My heart swelled for a moment, *are my parents here?*

The sight I saw enter through the doorway was most unexpected. I took a moment to let the shock register. Atzi was standing in front of me with her hands bound together like mine, but she was led by Necalli, who held a candle in his other hand. I was surprised by the dim light, and I could think of nothing but to stare at both of them while Necalli shut the door behind me. With the candle, I saw that the Warrior outside of my window had taken a new post. I didn't like the way this looked.

"What are you doing?" I asked. I was shocked when Atzi shed the rope as if it was never around her wrists at all.

She smiled brightly at my shocked face, "Miss me?"

"We don't have a lot of time." Necalli interrupted, "I told them to give us some privacy, but they won't be gone long."

"They listen to you?" I asked.

"Sometimes," Necalli admitted. "You two need to go."

"Go? Go where?"

"Anywhere." Atzi said quickly, "I don't plan on dying anytime soon, and neither should you."

"You're getting us out of here?" I asked Necalli.

He nodded, "I didn't know what they were planning. I wouldn't have taken you to my father if I knew what the Elders were planning."

"You could've listened to us. We told you it was dangerous."

Atzi talked over me, "Come on, we can live in the forest. We know what to eat, you've seen your father make weapons your entire life. It's safer to take our chances out there than to die in this village."

"The forest? The one that's full of monsters ready to devour us? What about the Bird?"

"It doesn't matter." Necalli interrupted. From his position by the window, he looked worried. "If you're going to go, now's your chance."

"Come on, Mila." Atzi walked over to me and cut my hands free with a knife I'd never seen her use before. I was surprised by how shaky I was when I stood. Atzi grabbed my arm, "Let's go."

"What about Necalli?" I asked her.

We both turned to look at him, but he didn't move his gaze from something outside the window. "I'll do what I have to," he said. He was still not looking at us. "Go."

Atzi didn't wait for him to tell us again. She pulled me out the door before I could even thank him. It was only when we were at the forest's edge that I turned around to look at the home I didn't think I'd see again. If I imagined that the sun was out and people were walking around the village, it was almost as if we were heading to our spot by the river instead of escaping. I wish things were that simple now.

Chapter Twelve

The forest was the reincarnation of all my nightmares put together into one dark setting. My eyes darted around uncontrollably from the ground to the sky. I tripped over the dangerous roots of bloodthirsty trees and stumbled into low branches that were waiting to pull me into the hidden corners of the night. The moon sent little light through this part of the forest. It was quiet -- dangerously so. Only our loud breathing seemed to disrupt the silent night.

The animals all seemed to be deep in sleep; we weren't disturbing them. *Are there animals in this part of the forest?* I felt eyes following us everywhere. I tried to see into the darkness, but each time my eyes found nothing, I felt a deeper sense of dread. Was this a good idea? Could we really survive on our own? We ducked under branches poised to snatch us and jumped through bushes trying to entangle us. It was hard work, especially in the dark, but we didn't dare stop or slow down. How long did we have before the Warriors would come after us?

We were long past the world we have always known. I couldn't hear the sound of the river anymore, and these woods felt especially intimidating. For a second, we risk catching our breath, but then we heard a strange sound in the night that made us start running again. I don't know when, but at some point, Atzi stopped leading me and let go of my hand. Now, I was running as fast as I could behind her, pushing myself to move faster so I didn't fall behind. I felt as if I was running so fast I must be flying, but there was always the reassuring feeling of the ground below me, keeping me steady.

We had to stop when the ground began sloping up too quickly for us to keep up our pace.

The hill before us was big, steep, and a tangle of tree roots and vines just waiting to trap us. The foliage was thick and everywhere we turned, making it hard to see where the bushes ended and the grass began. Atzi leaned up against a small tree to catch her breath again. I bent over with my hands on my knees.

It took a while before either of us could speak. Atzi was the first to catch her breath, "Do you know where we are? Do you recognize anything?"

I shook my head, "No."

"We should rest for an hour or so to get back some energy. I'm tired."

"Won't the Warriors be coming after us?"

"Not until morning."

"You seem confident."

"Necalli didn't want us to die -- none of the Warriors did. He said he would convince them not to report us. They'll only come after us when the Chief finds us missing in the morning."

"Won't they get in trouble if they agree?"

She shrugged, "Possibly. Necalli didn't really say anything, but I trust him."

I stood up and turned my thoughts to the path ahead of us, "Assuming we don't die before morning, what's your plan?"

"We keep running until we find somewhere safe. We can start our own two-man village."

"And if we run into a monster or animal before then?"

"You still believe in monsters?" She tried that smile that always worked back home but somehow falls flat out here on our own. "They're myths to keep us inside the village. All we have to worry about are the animals."

We sat on the ground in an exhausted silence. Atzi looked almost peaceful with her back to a tree and her eyes fighting to stay open. Eventually, I lay down with my eyes toward the sky so I could count stars until I fall asleep. I saw the patterns of the gods, and it made me remember the nights when Etapalli would take us out late so the stories she told would be accompanied with pictures. I forgot I was sitting in the middle of an unknown, terrifying forest. Everything felt peaceful right now. I had no trouble letting my eyes close.

***

When I woke up, I knew I shouldn't have fallen asleep. Something was terribly wrong. The forest was not as quiet as it was when I fell asleep. Serenity was replaced by the loudest noise I had ever heard. My chest felt like a drum, and my heart beat fast in blind panic. I jumped up from the ground, looking around. Atzi was frozen in her position, stunned into stillness. She looked confused, too -- a side-effect from being woken from a deep sleep. I snapped to my senses and looked above me, hoping that I had only awakened from a nightmare and terrified Atzi with my wild antics. It pained me how wrong I was.

The Bird was here, and it was right above us.

I didn't have the ability to scream. It was as if I never had a voice at all. I turned to look at Atzi for what to do, but she still hadn't moved. She was frozen. She was not going to move. *Hide.* My instincts took over, and I dove for the bushes. I thought running would only draw the Birds attention to me, so I busied myself with making sure I was absolutely hidden. It took only a few heartbeats to make sure I was safe, but it felt as if hours had passed by the time I was done. Without warning, a bright light flooded my vision, and for a moment, I was blind.

Then my eyes adjusted, and I saw that the lights were pointed to my right. They were pointed at Atzi. She still hadn't moved, but now she was looking up toward the sky. I faintly saw the shape of the Bird above us, and I realized that it wasn't moving at all. *How is it doing that?* The light started to get brighter. It burned my eyes, but I made myself focus on Atzi. She needed to move. *Why won't she move?* The lights were growing too bright now. I couldn't take it anymore.

I closed my eyes and covered them with my hands. I faintly heard a sound that wasn't the overpowering buzzing, but I couldn't make out what it was. *What's happening?* All I could think of was the buzzing and the white light that was still growing brighter. It was too bright for my hands to keep out of my eyes, and I felt such an intense heat that I believed the entire forest to be on fire. Then, in a single moment, it was all gone.

I was left with an intimidating darkness as my eyes re-adjust to my surroundings, and I was painfully aware of how loud my breathing was compared to the absolute silence of the forest around me. I thought I was going crazy. The trees reached out for me; the eyes of the night creatures woke up to stalk me. I was alone. *How am I alone?*

It took Atzi.

I didn't know what to do. I hardly felt the tears streaming down my face as I rose to my feet. I used a nearby tree to steady myself. *What do I do?* I couldn't continue on, not by myself -- not without Atzi. I couldn't survive without her. *Where did she go? What can I do?* Is this what the Bird does? Does it take people? What did it do to my friend? *Will it come back?* The buzzing was gone. Was I safe now? *Where's Atzi? What do I do?*

What *could* I do? It was hard to think. I couldn't go forward by myself. *I have to go back.* The villagers might be surprised to see me, but I couldn't do anything else now. I would tell them what I saw.

They could help me. They had to help me. I had just witnessed what this Bird does. They needed my information -- they needed me like they did when we first saw the Bird. I could give them information, and they could help me in return.

I ran back the way I came. The eyes that seemed to follow me earlier were now staring at me, unblinking. My tears made be blind, and I was running into trees and through thick bushes in my haste. At some point, I tripped and hit the ground hard; the wind was knocked out of me, and I had to sit for a moment to catch my breath. When nothing came except a pain in my head, I forced myself to stand. *Keep going.* I was unsteady, but I pushed forward.

I don't think Atzi and I got very far in our escape because it felt like it took no time for me to run into a group of Warriors. They were running towards me, but I think they intended to run in the direction of the Bird. I saw Necalli leading the group; he was surprised to see me. Without thinking, I ran into him, and he grabbed my shoulders as I cried harder now that I could breathe more easily.

"What are you doing here?" His angry voice demanded an answer.

"It took her! It took Atzi!" It was all I could say before my legs gave way and I hit the forest floor. Necalli came down with me, making my hard collapse easier. I realized someone was yelling and running toward the village, but I didn't care who it was. The Bird took Atzi, and I had no idea what would happen now.

***

I was restrained. No one seemed to care about what I had seen. Warriors held each of my arms and were guiding me through the village. The villagers didn't open their doors, but if they could, they stared through their windows. I couldn't tell exactly where we were going, but I knew it isn't Necalli leading me. He was somewhere behind me -- close, but too far away for me to feel safe. We continued to stumble through the poorly lit village before reaching a house close to its center.

Etapalli opened the door for us to enter through, and the room I walked into was dim, but full of life. There were many people here -- a mix of Elders and Warriors armed with spears and words. The Chief sat behind a fire, staring into the flames as if he were either thinking or sleeping. When he saw me, he didn't look surprised. He just looked tired. He sat up straighter, but didn't stand.

"Mila," He greeted me.

I couldn't respond. I didn't know how.

"You came back."

He knows I left? I try to look around for Necalli, but he had maneuvered his way to his mother's side. He was not looking at me.

"Explain," The Chief commanded.

If this were earlier in the day, I would have defied him and not spoken at all. But my confidence seemed to have disappeared with Atzi. I crumbled under his intensity and told him everything. I told him about Atzi visiting me with a Warrior after the sun fell, but I made sure not to mention the Warrior by name. I could tell that the Elders were intrigued by someone disobeying orders, but I didn't let anything slip about Necalli, not after he tried to help us escape. I told everyone how Atzi and I ran until we couldn't breathe and then took a moment to rest in a small clearing that couldn't have even been as big as the room we were in.

I told them about the Bird. I had to push myself to tell this story. If I stopped, how would I start again? The Warriors looked down when I spoke of how I hid in the bushes so the Bird wouldn't see me. When I talked about the brightest light I'd ever seen, they all looked skeptical. Even Necalli, the boy who helped me and had no reason to doubt me, looked as if he were trying to decide if I was telling the truth. I finished my story quickly, ending with running into a stunned Necalli just outside of the village. I wiped some stray tears off my face. *They have to help me now.*

The Chief looked back and forth between two Elders on opposite sides of his home: one who is a Warrior and one I recognized as the man who spoke out at the Meeting House. He addressed the Warrior first, "Send out a small party to see if you can find the girl. The light might've scared her away."

I wanted to shout out how ridiculous that sounded, but the grip on my right arm tightened and I kept my mouth shut. I watched as the elder Warrior told three others to join him. I didn't like the looks of the Elder that was left. He didn't look pleasant, and his stare made me shiver.

Once the group of Warriors had left, the Chief addressed the other Elder. "What do you think?"

I don't like this.

"I think the gods have delivered our lamb back to us." He was so calm and sincere that the others in the room immediately nodded at his words. They acted like they were all thinking the same thing. I didn't have the heart to look at Etapalli and Necalli. What if they believed him too? I made myself focus on the Chief, who was looking into the fire. *Please.*

"After all this child has paid, you still want her to give the ultimate price?" The Chief had a tone that neither helped nor condemned me. *Maybe my prayers are being heard.*

"She is a criminal who ran away from her sentence. In your father's time, this would be treason of the highest account!"

"I am not my father."

"No, you aren't." I didn't think this was meant to be a compliment. "You are our Chief, bound to protect this village and its people. It's your job to sentence this child as the gods see fit."

"I don't think the gods see murder as the highest form of the law."

"Then why would they give us this child, who has broken the law, back to us after she ran away from her sentence? The gods clearly want justice!"

"I am the Chief. I am the interpreter of the gods and their holy word, not you." He stood suddenly, "I am not my father, but I am the elected leader of this village, and my word is the word of the gods. Yesterday, your words were able to work their way into my mind, but not tonight. Tonight, I see clearly."

"So you will risk the lives of your people for the sake of this defiant child?" The room was silent. *Please.*

"She will be punished, but it won't be my hand that kills her. I have too much blood on my hands for that."

The fire seemed to glow brighter, like the gods themselves were confident in their choice for the winner of this power struggle. The old man backed down, stepping away with his head bowed in respect. Everyone in the room had finality written on their faces, but I couldn't believe that this was it. If I wasn't to be killed, but I have to be punished, then what will happen to me?

Chapter Thirteen

Exile. It would not be the Chief's hands that kill me, but his words. He announced his verdict as the sun was rising above the sky and the entire village stood gathered in front of us. We were in the Meeting House, which had been opened just for the show of strength and unity. I was in front of the villagers and near the Chief, who was standing alone on his pedestal. Warriors were gathered around me to ensure that I didn't try to escape again. *I couldn't get passed the entire village on my own with the sun shining.* I felt the heat of familiar eyes leering at me, and I wish I had the strength to meet their gaze. Instead, my eyes stayed locked on the floor.

The Chief read out my sentence like it was a call to arms. I was a curse upon this village, a plague to my family's' name. To pay for the crimes I committed, I had to face the consequences the gods bestowed upon me. In his infinite mercy, the Chief decided that it would *only* be the gods that decided my fate. I was to be escorted from the village by Warriors who were instructed to kill me if I tried to escape. My eyes were to be covered so I could not find my way home. I was to be released and sent off into the forest by myself, where I must rely on the gods to keep me alive.

I was not allowed to say goodbye to my parents -- that was one of the few requirements the Elders couldn't live without. After they decided on a punishment that would make me an example to the village, they agreed that talking to my parents would only promote distrust. I didn't agree, but there was nothing I could say to change their minds. *What will happen to me if I wound their pride now? I may not survive my exile, but I don't want to put my parents through any more pain. I can't let my actions hurt them anymore.*

I didn't see my parents as I passed through the congregation. I searched for them, careful not to miss any faces. The longer I looked, the more confident I became that they were not in the Meeting House. I saw Etapalli sitting by herself in the crowd. If Zolin were still here, Necalli would be by her side instead of standing silently in a group of younger Warriors. If Zolin were still here, none of this would be happening. Etapalli didn't look at me, so I can't even pretend to know what she's thinking. I saw the older woman whom I had seen sewing the black flower. She looked into my eyes, holding my gaze longer than I thought anyone would dare. I thought I saw her nod at me, but she was too quick for me to be certain.

The Warriors were quick to place a bag over my head so I wouldn't be able to see where we were going. I thought it was ridiculous to lead me through a forest if I couldn't even see what was in front of me, but I was not exactly in any position to argue, "Sorry if I fall," I announced to no one in particular. "It's hard to walk when you can't see."

I didn't hear a response. I was pushed to the side, forced to wait for the Chief to join us. It took longer than I thought it would. *What are they doing?* I panicked for a moment, worried that they might march the villagers by me in my vulnerable state for one last show of power. *They wouldn't, would they?* What if my parents were in there? I couldn't stand for them to see me like this. Feet stop in front of me. The world seems to stop.

"Let's go." I recognized the Chief's commanding tone. I was pushed forward. Immediately, it was clear that the trek ahead of me would be a long one. I let my mind wander to pass the time and tried to calm my nerves.

What will I do? How will I survive? I'm a good scavenger, but what if the forest was too different from what I'm used to? I couldn't survive in unfamiliar terrain. If I didn't know what was edible, then I had no chance. And what if there wasn't water nearby? I'd always lived with the river at my doorstep. I knew I couldn't live long without water. What if I was taken away from the river and there wasn't any water nearby? What would I do? *It's a forest. There has to be rain.* And food? What would I do if I can't eat? *You can do this. You'll be fine.*

I started to wonder where my parents were. Are they allowed to cry for me? *I miss them.* I thought about my father, the man who can hardly climb the ladder every night to sleep. He sits diligently in his corner to make weapons, playing his part in the village. Then there's my mother, the woman who taught me almost everything I know. She always protected me. Had I let her down? Did she hate me? I wished I could talk to her and settle things properly. I wished I had told them the truth when I had the chance. If I had told them the truth, would we be safe together in the village right now or would they be exiled with me?

We walked for what seemed like forever. I didn't know how long we'd been going, and I didn't know how much longer we had to go. I stumbled and fell, but someone always caught me. Occasionally, I could hear muttering from ahead of me, but it was never loud enough for me to hear the words. With each step, a new fear rose in me that I couldn't shake away. Something about this march into the unknown gave me a very strange feeling.

***

It was an eternity before we finally stopped. "Let her see." the Chief commanded. It took a moment before the bag was removed from my head. I had become so accustomed to the darkness, that the sudden light, even though it was dim, made me grimace. When I finally adjusted to my surroundings, my mouth fell open.

The sun was low in the sky, and the world is black. Everything around me was scorched from a great catastrophe from which this forest had yet to heal. I could hardly see any green around me. *This is where they're leaving me. They want me to die.* My hand covered my mouth as I searched around for any sign of life. I would take my forest over this nightmare. I felt like begging for my forest now.

"Men," the Chief commanded. I was pushed in front of a line of Warriors that now had their spears pointed toward me. I searched every face for mercy; I found nothing. "This is to make sure you don't try to follow us home. Go."

I was too afraid to cry; too afraid to beg. This was all too sudden. Far too real. I raced into the destruction, hoping that there was life somewhere on the other side of this great expanse. The sun cast shadows of too many half-burned trees for me to be sure that there was life anywhere nearby, but I didn't let that stop me. I *couldn't* let that stop me. I was too afraid of what lay behind me to care about what waited ahead.

I ran until I couldn't breathe. There were no obstacles in my path this time; everything in my path was either dead or dying. Occasionally, I glimpsed some small sign of life, but nothing that could support me. Even when the sun slowly began to disappear behind the earth, I didn't stop to rest. There was no life here to scare me, but there was nothing to hide me, either. I don't know how far I traveled because everything still looked the same. It wasn't not until the sun started to rise that I finally collapsed with exhaustion. There was nothing here to save me.

It Came from the Sky

***

All I do is wander. The sun rises, and I begin my day. There is no food as far as I can see. I stop to rest often. There is no water. My stomach aches from emptiness and my head starts to spin if I move too quickly. I welcome the night, even though I know it is when I'm the most vulnerable. In the dark, fear keeps my mind off of my empty stomach. I can only sleep in little moments at a time.

The sun has risen three times in my exile, but I don't think it will rise a fourth time. I seem to fall every time I try to stand, so I sit most of the day. There is no water around me. There is no food. There is no life, only a few burnt trees and some dead grass. I've never felt so alone in my life. Sometimes, I think I hear my name, and I use the little energy I have left to look for their voice. Once, I thought I saw my mother. When I ran to her, I fell through her apparition onto the hard ground.

The sun is beginning to set now. It looks breathtaking. The sky is a painting of orange, red, and yellow. There isn't a cloud in the sky. Even though I hate this forest around me, I lie on my back with my arms spread out beside me. The sky starts morphing into the most intense pink I've ever seen. I don't want this picture to end.

I think the pounding in my ears is growing louder, reaching a deafening crescendo that feels as if it's echoing throughout the entire forest. I try to breathe in time to the beating, but it speeds up past my capabilities. It occurs to me that the beating isn't my heart at all, but an unnatural buzzing coming from the sky. I'm afraid, but not like I used to be. I'm too tired to move. I *can't* move.

So, when I see the Bird fly above me, I don't say a word. The sun is sinking below the earth, and I don't want to miss a moment of it. My eyes feel heavy, and I think I might actually be able to sleep through the night. Not even the bright light from the Bird is enough to keep me awake. I close my eyes, and I feel like I'm in complete darkness. *It's peaceful here.* I keep my eyes closed.

17151065R00120

Printed in Great Britain
by Amazon